THE GREAT CHILI KILL-OFF

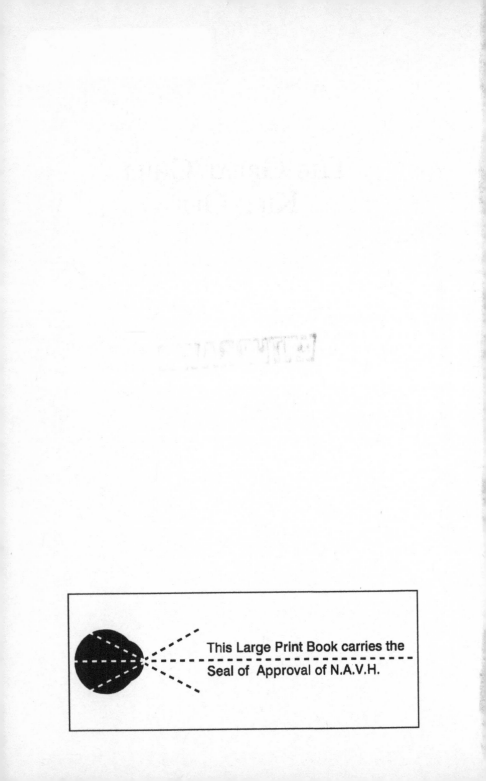

This Large Print Book carries the
Seal of Approval of N.A.V.H.

A FRESH BAKED MYSTERY

THE GREAT CHILI KILL-OFF

LIVIA J. WASHBURN

WHEELER PUBLISHING
A part of Gale, a Cengage Company

GALE
A Cengage Company

Farmington Hills, Mich • San Francisco • New York • Waterville, Maine
Meriden, Conn • Mason, Ohio • Chicago

Copyright © 2017 by Livia J. Washburn.
Wheeler Publishing, a part of Gale, a Cengage Company.

LIBRARY OF CONGRESS CIP DATA ON FILE.
CATALOGUING IN PUBLICATION FOR THIS BOOK
IS AVAILABLE FROM THE LIBRARY OF CONGRESS

ISBN-13: 978-1-4328-4780-7 (softcover)

Published in 2018 by arrangement with Livia J. Washburn

Printed in Mexico
1 2 3 4 5 6 7 22 21 20 19 18

Dedicated to my husband, James, and my daughters, Joanna and Shayna. I hit the lottery when it comes to family.

CHAPTER 1

Sam Fletcher took his right hand off the steering wheel, reached over, and thumped the pickup's dashboard.

"Dadgum GPS," he said.

A disembodied voice replied, *"In one hundred yards, take the next exit and turn left at the stop sign."*

"That's not the best way to go," Sam insisted.

From the passenger seat, Phyllis Newsom said, "It's a navigation system, you know, not an old TV set that you can get to work again by hitting it on the side."

"Hey, that method worked at least half the time, and when it didn't, you could pull the tubes out and take 'em down to the drugstore and test 'em on the tube tester they had there. Just because a TV stopped workin', that didn't mean you threw it away and bought a new one, the way folks do now."

"Exit here and turn left at the stop sign," the navigation system said.

"But that'll take us fifty miles out of our way!" Sam's foot pressed down harder on the accelerator and the pickup, as well as the travel trailer it was pulling, zoomed past the exit and remained on the Interstate.

"You realize you're shouting at the GPS, don't you?" Phyllis asked.

Sam tightened both hands on the steering wheel. "Well, I, for one, am not ready to welcome our new navigation system overlords."

In the back seat of the extended cab pickup, Eve Turner looked over at Carolyn Wilbarger and asked, "What's he talking about?"

Carolyn let out a snort. "I've long since given up trying to understand half of what that man says."

The pickup, with a camper top attached over its bed and the travel trailer behind it, continued heading west on the Interstate. After a while, the GPS gave up on telling Sam to turn around and go back to the state highway he had passed and instead announced, *"Recalculating."*

"I guess I'm like most fellas," Sam said. "I'm a little touchy about bein' told I don't know where I'm goin'."

Phyllis smiled and said, "You think?"

A grin stretched across Sam's rugged, weatherbeaten face. "You'll see I'm right, though, when we get there," he said.

"How much longer is that going to be?" Carolyn asked. "I never have liked long road trips. I get too stiff when I sit for hours and hours."

"Well, when you're headin' for West Texas, it's gonna be a long trip. There's just no gettin' around that. Everywhere out there is a long way from anywhere else." Sam glanced at the rear-view mirror and met Carolyn's eyes in it. "I guess if you want, I can stop for a minute and you can climb back there in the War Wagon to stretch out, although you're really not supposed to ride in a travel trailer while it's movin'."

"No, that's all right," Carolyn said. "We'll be stopping for gas at some point, and I can get out and walk around a little then."

"All right, but with the double tank I've got on this pickup, it may be a while."

"But we can stop any time anyone needs to," Phyllis said. "There's no real rush to get to Cactus Bluff, as long as we're there by tomorrow evening for the opening festivities." She paused, then repeated, "The War Wagon?"

"You know, like that John Wayne movie

we watched a while back."

"Yes, I know, but that's a travel trailer we're pulling, not an armored stagecoach full of gold." Phyllis frowned. "You're not planning on mounting a Gatling gun on top of it, are you? I'm not sure Molly and Frank would like that."

"Don't worry, I'll get it back to 'em in just as good a shape as it was when we borrowed it," Sam assured her.

Phyllis hoped that would be the case. Molly and Frank Dobson were good friends of hers, dating back to her teaching days. They were about ten years younger than her, so they were still in harness while Phyllis had been retired for that long. Molly taught American History at the high school, which had also been Phyllis's subject on the eighth grade level, while Frank coached and taught algebra.

When Sam first came up with the idea of attending — and entering — the annual Great Chili Cook-Off in Cactus Bluff, he had planned to rent a giant motor home for the trip. Phyllis had thought of Molly and Frank and their travel trailer, though, and suggested that Sam at least check with them about borrowing it. Since it was summer, it was possible the Dobsons might be using the trailer, but that hadn't turned out to be the case.

Now the War Wagon, as Sam had dubbed it, was rolling along behind his pickup. Once they got to Cactus Bluff, he would bunk in the back of the pickup under the camper top while the three ladies shared the trailer. So that had turned out well.

Phyllis could only hope the rest of the trip would go as smoothly.

A short time later, Sam nodded toward an old, abandoned building slowly falling into ruins on the left side of the Interstate and said, "Poor old Stuckey's. I stopped there many a time to buy gas and get a hamburger and a malt while I was drivin' back and forth on this road. Always stopped any time I came across a Stuckey's, in fact. And now they're all gone, as far as I know. You wouldn't think a business as successful as they seemed to be could just disappear like that."

"Nothing stays the same forever," Phyllis said. "No matter how much it seems like it should."

From the back seat, Carolyn said, "When you get to be our age, you realize that all over again every day."

Eve said, "Oh, I don't know. I think it's more of a state of mind. Or heart, rather. Sam and I are young at heart, aren't we,

Sam? We look at change as something new and exciting, not something to be regretted."

"Mostly," Sam agreed. "I do miss those Stuckey's hamburgers, though."

"I think we've all had more than our share of excitement in our lives," Carolyn said. "It's time for peace and quiet."

With a smile, Eve said, "Yes, dear, but you were born with an old soul."

"There probably won't be much peace and quiet at this thing we're going to," Phyllis said. "From what I've read about it, it's sort of a celebration."

"Woodstock for chili," Sam said. "Or Burnin' Man."

Carolyn sniffed. "You mean a gathering of degenerates."

"I wouldn't go quite *that* far," Phyllis said.

But any time thousands of people crowded into an area that was usually almost deserted, bent on having a good time, a lot of things went on, and not all of them had to do with cooking chili. A country music concert was scheduled as part of the opening festivities, and from what Phyllis had read, there were a lot of impromptu musical performances all weekend. Jam sessions, people used to call them, but she didn't know if anyone still used that term.

The cook-off was also like a family reunion in one sense, because many of the competitors knew each other quite well and had been matching their chili recipes for a long time. Of course, there were always newcomers, too, like Sam would be this year. She hoped he wouldn't be too disappointed if he didn't fare well in the competition.

She was used to not winning. She and Carolyn had competed for many years in baking and other cooking and recipe contests, and anyone who took part in such competitions on a regular basis was liable to lose more often than they won. Sam was a relative newbie at such things, though. But he believed in his chili recipe, and as his friend, Phyllis intended to support him all the way, no matter what.

A short time later they stopped for a break, since Carolyn wasn't the only one who needed to stretch her legs. Sam topped off the gas in the pickup while Eve bought some snacks in the convenience store where they had stopped. Then it was back on the road.

Cactus Bluff was in far West Texas, between the Davis Mountains and the Big Bend. Drivable in a day . . . but it would be a long day. That was why they had started early. Phyllis had offered to help Sam with the driving, and he had promised to let her take over if he needed her to, but she knew he planned to handle all of it if he could.

"Why in the world would they have a big competition in a ghost town?" Carolyn asked. "Wouldn't it be better if they held it in some place with more . . . amenities?"

"Yes, like a resort hotel," Eve added.

"Well, from what I've read, there's a hotel in Cactus Bluff," Sam replied, "but it's not what you'd call a resort. Been there since the late 1800s, when the settlement was a boomtown for a little while because of the mining in the area. It was one of the biggest towns between San Antonio and El Paso, but only for a year or so. Then the mines petered out and folks started movin' away. Now there's not much left . . . except on the weekend closest to the Fourth of July every year. That's when they have the chili cook-off."

"Didn't they used to hold the cook-off somewhere else?" Phyllis said.

"That was a different cook-off," Sam said. "Fella named Hiram Boudreau started this one, and it took off. Brings in folks from all over the world, I've heard, and it's been on TV some."

Phyllis was well aware of that. The contest's fame had helped her pitch the idea

14

for a story about it to her editor at *A Taste of Texas,* the magazine for which she wrote a monthly column. This chili cook-off was a big enough deal that it would need more than a column devoted to it, however. The editor had decided it deserved a feature story, and the prospect of writing that made Phyllis more than a little nervous. When she had retired from teaching, the thought that someday she might be a magazine writer had never entered her mind.

But she had never anticipated that she would wind up solving murders, either, and . . . well . . . look how *that* had turned out.

Sam had a stubborn streak, but he had a practical side to go with it, so that afternoon he asked Phyllis to drive for a few hours. She was glad he was being reasonable. For one thing, she didn't want him falling asleep at the wheel, and for another, he didn't need to wear himself out. None of them were as young as they used to be. All four of them had been retired from teaching for quite a while, sharing the big old house on a quiet, tree-lined residential street in Weatherford. Officially it was her house and the other three were renting rooms from her, but as far as Phyllis was concerned, they were all family.

They switched back and Sam took the wheel again late in the afternoon, after they had stopped for an early supper. They left the Interstate and headed southwest on a smaller state highway. It would still be several hours before they reached Cactus Bluff, but luckily at this time of year, with the summer solstice only a week or so behind them, the sun didn't set until quite late, especially this far west. If nothing happened to delay them, they would reach their destination before it got dark.

"Are those mountains?" Carolyn asked as she pointed between Phyllis and Sam, through the pickup's windshield. "I thought they were just clouds on the horizon at first, but now I'm not sure."

"Nope, not clouds," Sam said. "Those are the Davis Mountains. We'll skirt around the east side of 'em. Maybe on the way back you ladies'd like to go through 'em and see McDonald Observatory and Fort Davis."

"Would there be a good place to stay?" Eve asked. "Some kind of resort, maybe?"

"Well, I don't know. A lot of tourists come out here, so there are probably some decent places."

"We'll think about it," Phyllis said. "I've

never been to the restored fort, and you know historical things always interest me."

"Oh, my goodness, look over there," Carolyn said suddenly. She pointed again. Several hundred yards off the highway, out on some dry flats bordering a range of hills, a number of small, tan funnel clouds had sprung into existence. They whirled and skipped across the ground as if they were performing some sort of intricate ballet.

"Dust devils," Sam said. "We see 'em now and then up at home, but they're more common out here. Sort of like miniature tornadoes that don't pack near as much punch."

"I know what dust devils are," Carolyn said. "But I've never seen that many of them together. It's impressive . . . in a stark, desolate sort of way."

"A lot of West Texas is like that," Sam agreed.

The red ball of the sun gradually slipped down the western sky. The mountains loomed larger, then fell away behind as the travelers never actually reached them. The peaks remained visible, though, as did other ranges of small mountains scattered all around.

The navigation system spoke up again, instructing Sam to turn onto a smaller paved road that angled off to the south from the state highway. This time he followed the suggestion. The pickup's tires made a bumping sound against the rough joints in the macadam surface.

"Are you sure this is the right way?" Carolyn asked. "This road doesn't look like it leads anywhere."

"Isn't this the way a lot of horror movies start out?" Eve added.

"This is the way the GPS said to go," Sam told them.

"Yes," Carolyn replied, "but you said you didn't trust the thing!"

Sam smiled and said, "Don't worry, we're headin' the right way. I studied the map real good before we ever started. At least this road's paved . . . sort of. There are plenty out here that aren't."

The smaller road wound through low, rocky hills. In places the route was cut through bluffs and ridges, so that rough walls loomed on both sides of the vehicle. They rattled over a couple of old plank bridges spanning deep, dry washes. Phyllis thought the landscape looked a lot like that in the Western movies Sam loved so much.

The sun was still hanging just above the mountains to the west when the pickup went through a saddle in some rolling hills and the road dropped down a long slope into a broad valley.

"There it is," Sam said. "Cactus Bluff."

"Oh, my," Phyllis said.

CHAPTER 2

The business district of the settlement consisted of only a dozen permanent buildings, plus the abandoned ruins of several others, Phyllis saw as Sam started the pickup down the slope into the valley. A couple of those unpaved roads he had mentioned came in at angles and crossed the road they were on, showing that at one time Cactus Bluff had been the center of whatever traffic there was in this area. Some old frame houses were on those smaller roads.

Still standing along the paved road were a couple of fairly substantial-looking brick buildings, several weathered frame structures, and a couple that appeared to be old-fashioned adobe. Slightly off to one side was a small mobile home park with a dozen of what Phyllis had grown up hearing referred to as trailer houses, all of them with skirting around the bottom and small yards that made them look like they were there to stay.

At the moment, however, the town of Cactus Bluff's most dominant feature was a huge open-sided tent with broad stripes of red, white, and blue on its canvas top, just on the other side of what passed for the downtown area. It was almost the size of a football field, Phyllis estimated as she studied it.

"Is that tent where they have the cook-off?" Carolyn asked.

"I reckon it must be," Sam said. "The judgin' and the show parts, anyway. I think most of the cookin' takes place outside, where the contestants are parked. You know, like tailgatin' at a football game or NAS-CAR race."

Smaller tents were set up around the larger one. Phyllis didn't know what their purpose was, but she supposed she would find out. There was also a long row of portable toilets, as well as more of the distinctively green, phone-booth-shaped contraptions placed here and there.

Dozens of motor homes and travel trailers were parked in several rows that formed a semi-circle around the tents. Parking spaces for the recreational vehicles had been marked off with stakes and ropes. Plenty of pickups, SUVs, vans, and cars were wedged into a large gravel-surfaced parking area, as well. Once Sam's pickup had emerged from the hills so that Phyllis had a good view of the valley where Cactus Bluff was located, she was able to see four or five more vehicles ahead of them on the old road, obviously bound for the same destination she and her friends were.

"It looks like a boomtown again," she said.

Sam nodded. "Yeah. It will be for the next few days. But then, come Monday mornin', the place'll be mostly deserted again."

Carolyn said, "This place is so far off the beaten path, how does anyone who lives here make a living?"

"From what I've read, many of them are retirees, so they don't have to," Phyllis said. "There's a little grocery store and a gas station, and a hotel for tourists who stop here on their way to the Big Bend, so there's some business going on. Also, there's a small clinic. People come seventy or eighty or even a hundred miles for medical attention."

"What do they do for internet service?" Eve asked.

"Satellite dishes," Sam said. "That's the only thing that would work this far out."

"It's strange, isn't it," Phyllis said, "how for more than half of our lives, that ques-

22

tion wouldn't have even existed, and now it seems vitally important."

"It is important," Sam said. "Folks got to stay connected."

Carolyn blew out a slightly contemptuous breath. She knew how to use the internet but had never really succumbed to its temptations. "They used to stay connected with letters and the telephone."

"Like we were talkin' about earlier, times change."

There was no red light in Cactus Bluff, not even a stop sign, but as the road leveled out and approached the town, Phyllis saw a sign advising motorists that the speed limit was 30 miles per hour.

"Better be careful," she told Sam with a smile. "This might be a speed trap up ahead."

They passed a boxy Jeep with lights mounted on its roof and a sign on the door that read CONSTABLE. Sam had already slowed down to the speed limit.

The parking lot at Boudreau's Market was full. People were waiting in line at the gas pumps on one side of the lot. Men in Hawaiian shirts and women in t-shirts and shorts walked in and out of the Boudreau Hotel and strolled on both sides of the street. Plenty of gimme caps and cowboy hats were in evidence. Nearly everyone wore sunglasses, despite the fact that the sun was almost down. Traffic on the road moved at a crawl because of all the pedestrians cutting between the vehicles. Phyllis saw a few kids and dogs but was surprised there weren't more. She supposed that the chili cook-off wasn't really that much of a family activity.

"There's a mob of people here," Carolyn said. "I don't like mobs."

"Once we get where we're goin' and get parked, it won't be so bad," Sam told her. "You can always hide out in the War Wagon any time you want to."

"Needing some privacy isn't the same as hiding out. Are we going to have electricity and plumbing?"

Sam shook his head and said, "There's a central dump station, but no hookups at each space. We've got a generator for electricity, though, and the water tanks are full, plus I can take the trailer and fill 'em up again if I need to. We'll have all the conveniences of home, just not as much room."

Carolyn muttered something. Phyllis couldn't make out the words, but she knew that her old friend was just blowing off steam. If it had been anything important, Carolyn would have made sure that they all understood quite clearly.

They had to drive all the way through town, what there was of it, to reach the gravel road that led past the big tent to the parking areas. A sign was posted with arrows painted on it pointing to various sections of reserved spaces designated by numbers.

"You reserved a space for us, didn't you?" Carolyn asked.

"You betcha," Sam said. "Did that the same time I signed up for the contest."

"I still say we can all pitch in to cover the costs of this trip," Phyllis said.

"Nope. This was my idea. The whole thing is my treat."

"Well, I know you're too stubborn to argue with . . . so all right. I won't bring it up again."

Sam was driving slowly through the parking area. He said, "Here we go," and turned at another sign indicating which spaces were on this row. The rows were set far enough apart so people could pull through the spaces and not have to back their motor homes or travel trailers into them. Skillfully, Sam maneuvered into the space he had reserved, which was marked with yet another sign, this one bearing the number 457, and slowed to a stop.

He turned to Phyllis and said, "You mind seein' if I'm lined up good?"

"Of course," she said. She opened her door and got out of the pickup. A quick look told her that Sam had brought the travel trailer to a halt in the very center of the space. Through the door she had left open, she called, "Perfect."

Sam put the pickup in park and turned off the engine. "Here we are, ladies," he said. "Our home for the next few days."

"Don't expect me to say home sweet home," Carolyn said.

"Oh, I wasn't."

Phyllis closed her door as Sam got out on the other side of the cab. Both of them went to the back of the pickup to start unhooking the travel trailer and getting it leveled and set up. They had practiced that several times before leaving Weatherford, so they knew what they were doing. Carolyn and Eve got out and stretched. To the west, the sun was an orange ball that had just touched the tops of the highest peaks in that direction.

Phyllis and Sam had been working for only a couple of minutes when a young, friendly voice said, "Hi, folks." Phyllis straightened from what she was doing and looked over her shoulder to see a young woman standing there with a clipboard.

The newcomer wore cowboy boots, but above them her long legs were bare up to an extremely short pair of cut-off jeans. She also wore a white button-up shirt with no sleeves and the tails tied up to reveal her belly. A straw cowboy hat rested on honey-colored hair that hung halfway down her back. The deep tan on her face and arms and legs testified that she spent most of her time outdoors.

The woman glanced at her clipboard and said to Sam, "Are you Mr. Fletcher?"

"That's right," Sam said. Phyllis gave him credit. He didn't seem to be paying too much attention to the fact that the top two buttons on the young woman's shirt were unfastened.

"Welcome to Cactus Bluff," she said. "I have a little bit of paperwork I need you to sign. It's just a standard liability waiver and a notice that you're responsible for your own belongings — and your behavior — while you're here."

"We promise not to act up too much," Sam said as he took the clipboard and pen she held out to him.

"I'm McKayla Carson. That's M-C-K-A-Y-L-A." She glanced at Phyllis, Carolyn, and Eve. "Is one of these ladies Mrs.

Fletcher?"

Sam had scrawled his signature on each of the sheets of paper where they were marked with an X. He handed the clipboard back and said, "No, they're . . . friends of mine."

"Oh. Okay."

Sam went on, "This is, uh, Phyllis . . . and Carolyn . . . and Eve."

McKayla smiled brightly at them. "Hello, ladies. I hope you and Sam enjoy your visit to Cactus Bluff. Remember, everybody is here to have a good time. Now, there are no officially scheduled activities tonight, although there'll probably be some music later on. But I'm sure the four of you can come up with your own fun." She handed Sam another paper. "Here's a map of the grounds. If you need anything, the office is over by the main tent. You won't have any trouble finding it. See you later!"

She turned and walked off.

Carolyn waited until McKayla was out of earshot before saying in a low, outraged voice, "Why, that shameless little hussy! She thinks that we're your . . . your harem or something, Sam!"

"Oh, I don't reckon she meant that," Sam said.

"Then why are you blushing, dear?" Eve asked.

"I'm not. I'm just, uh, gettin' a start on the sunburn I'll probably have before this weekend is over."

"And did you see the brazen way she was dressed?" Carolyn went on.

Phyllis said, "She's just a healthy, friendly young woman, from the looks of it. We really shouldn't judge people."

"You don't have to judge them if you don't want to," Carolyn said. "I'm quite comfortable with it, myself."

"What *are* we going to do for the rest of the evening?" Eve asked.

"After riding for so long, I'm tired. I may just go on to bed," Carolyn said.

Sam said, "I thought I might take a walk, have a look around. It'll feel good to move a little after sittin' all day."

"That sounds like a good idea to me," Phyllis said.

"I'll come with you," Eve added.

"Then I'll hold down the fort here," Carolyn said. "The place probably shouldn't be left unattended, anyway. There's no telling what kinds of people might be here in this crowd."

Sam sniffed the air. "The kind that like to cook chili, I'm thinkin', unless my nose is lyin' to me. Why don't you come with us, Carolyn? I'm sure it'll be all right."

Carolyn hesitated, then said, "Well . . . I suppose it *would* feel good to move around some more. As long as we're not out too late."

Phyllis and Sam finished setting up the travel trailer, then he drove the pickup out of the area for recreational vehicles and parked it in the gravel lot about a hundred yards away. By the time he had walked back to the travel trailer, Phyllis, Carolyn, and Eve were waiting for him.

"Shall we go, ladies?" he asked with a mock half-bow. The four of them walked toward the big tent. A lot of people were out and about as dusk settled down over the valley, bringing with it a hint of coolness after the heat of the day. The sun was behind the mountains now, but a majestic arch of red and gold rose over the peaks, shading to deep blue, then purple, then black the farther one looked to the east. It wouldn't be long before it was dark enough for the stars to start popping into view, Phyllis thought. She'd heard that night fell quickly out here, and she was about to see proof of that for herself.

Their route took them past a large, squarish truck with a couple of whip antennas and a satellite dish mounted on it. In the fading light, Phyllis saw the logo embellished on the side of the truck in garishly painted letters. *INSIDE BEAT,* it read, and as Phyllis realized what she was looking at, she caught her breath a little. Surely it wasn't possible —

"Mrs. Newsom!" someone exclaimed. "I had no idea you were going to be here."

Phyllis and the others stopped as a heavyset young man with thick glasses and a mop of dark hair hurried up to them. He went on, "When the boss decided to send us out here, I never dreamed we'd run into somebody we know."

"Howdy, Josh," Sam said. "Good to see you again, son. You still an intern for that TV show?"

A look of pride appeared on Josh Green's broad face. "Shoot, no," he said. "I'm a producer now. Well, an associate producer, but still, you know, I get paid and everything. And I get to make some of the decisions."

"Well, good for you," Sam told him. "I know that's what you had your sights set on."

"You said *we,*" Phyllis said. "Does that mean —"

A door on the side of the truck opened

and a woman in high heels, tight jeans, and a silk shirt descended a set of fold-down steps. She stopped short at the bottom of them, and while she was too self-possessed to stare, she did look a little surprised as she said, "Well, what do you know. If it isn't America's favorite cookie-baking, crime-busting grandma." Felicity Prosper brushed back her long brown hair and then couldn't stop her eyes from widening slightly as if something had just occurred to her. "OMG, are you here to solve another murder, Mrs. Newsom?"

CHAPTER 3

A year and a half earlier, a crew from the tabloid TV show *Inside Beat* had gotten mixed up in Phyllis's efforts to solve a murder committed during Weatherford's annual Christmas parade. Reporter Felicity Prosper, intern Josh Green, and cameraman/driver Nick Baker had all been in danger from the killer, as had Phyllis herself, before that case was wrapped up.

Phyllis hadn't seen any of them since the aftermath of that investigation, except for catching a glimpse of Felicity on the TV show every now and then, but since she wasn't a regular viewer of *Inside Beat,* that was rare.

She had to stop herself from wincing now at Felicity's eager question. She said, "No, there hasn't been any murder. We're just here so Sam can enter his chili recipe in the competition."

"You're going to be in the contest, Mr.

Fletcher? It's nice to see you, by the way."

"Good to see you, too, Ms. Prosper," Sam said. "Yep, I'm gonna try to impress the judges with the way I cook up a bowl of good ol' Texas red."

"You don't cook chili, Mrs. Newsom?" Josh asked.

"Well, I can, of course," Phyllis said, "but that's more in Sam's line. Carolyn, though, is going to enter a couple of the other contests that they're holding in conjunction with the main one."

"That's right," Carolyn said. "I have a recipe for gluten-free cornbread that's excellent, and I think I'm going to enter the competition for dishes made with left-over chili —"

Felicity interrupted her, bringing a scowl to Carolyn's face. "I thought for a minute there we might have stumbled on some real excitement," she said. "You have to admit, it was a reasonable assumption when I saw you, Mrs. Newsom. Murder *does* seem to follow you around."

"Oh, I think that's overstating the case —" Phyllis began.

"Really? How many killers have you caught?" Without giving Phyllis a chance to answer, Felicity went on, "See? There are so many you can't even come up with the number."

"Well, if you'll just give me a minute —"

"That's all right, I can have Josh look it up. It won't take him long. He's good at things like that. And I'll probably need the number for the story I'm going to do —"

This time it was Phyllis who did the interrupting. "There isn't any story," she said firmly. "We're just here for the chili cook-off and the other contests, as well as a little vacation. That's all."

"Just our way of celebratin' the Fourth of July this year," Sam put in.

"Yes, but something else could happen," Felicity insisted. "You never know."

"Oh, I don't think that's likely," Phyllis said. "Everybody is here to have a good time. No one is looking for trouble —"

An angry shout erupted from somewhere close by. Phyllis heard a thud that sounded like a fist striking flesh and bone, and as she turned to look toward the direction of the sound, she saw a man stumble backward from behind a motor home parked three or four spaces away.

From the looks of it, he was the one who had gotten punched. His feet tangled together and he lost his balance, falling heavily on his backside. As he lay there, another man rushed out from behind the motor home and came after him.

The second man drew back his foot to launch a vicious kick, but the first man rolled out of the way of it. Before the attacker could do anything else, a couple of men hurried up behind him and grabbed his arms.

"Take it easy, Kurt," one of them urged. "Hammersmith ain't worth it. You don't want to get yourself kicked outta the contest when you got a good chance of beatin' him this year."

"He's been sniffin' around Lindy again," the man called Kurt said as he pulled against the grips of the two men, who seemed to be friends of his. "You know what he's like. Damn tomcat always on the prowl!"

By now the man who had been knocked down was on his feet again, brushing himself off. He took hold of his chin and worked his jaw back and forth, evidently checking to see if anything was broken. Satisfied that it wasn't, he said, "You do me an injustice, old friend. I was just asking your wife about her health. Just a polite, friendly gesture, you know."

"You're not polite or friendly when it comes to women, Hammersmith," Kurt said. "You're a damn shark!"

"I thought I was a tomcat," Hammersmith said with a smile. "You'll have to make up your mind."

"Somebody get this son of a — Just get him out of my sight, all right?"

One of the men holding Kurt said, "You won't go after him if I let you go?"

For a second Kurt still looked like he wanted to continue the attack, but then he said, "No, you're right, he's not worth it."

"All right, then." The other man released Kurt's arm and stepped over to Hammersmith. "Get out of here while you still can."

"This is a common area," Hammersmith protested. "I have a right to be here."

"Just go, blast it! If you don't, none of us are gonna be responsible for you gettin' whipped."

Hammersmith held up slightly pudgy hands, palms out. He was a stocky man, just a little below medium height, with a ruddy face and curly brown hair. Phyllis estimated his age to be around fifty. He said, "All right, all right, I'm going. But I swear, I meant no harm. Anything between Lindy and myself is in the past. As long as that's the way she wants it, that is."

Kurt started to lunge at Hammersmith again. The man who had told Hammersmith to beat it grabbed Kurt's arm and he and his companion held Kurt back while Hammersmith turned to walk away.

His path took him toward Phyllis, Sam, Eve, Felicity Prosper, and Josh Green. He glanced at them, paused for a beat, and then his face lit up with a smile. He came forward with enthusiasm and an extended hand. Phyllis realized he was heading straight for Felicity.

"Well, hello there," he said. "I don't believe we've met. I'm Joe D. Hammersmith, defending and perennial champion of the Great Chili Cook-Off."

"Yes, I've heard of you, Mr. Hammersmith," Felicity said as she shook hands with the man. "You've won the competition for the past three years, haven't you?"

"That's why I said *perennial.* I intend to chalk up another win this year, too. And please, call me Joe D."

Carolyn nodded toward Sam and said, "This man right here might have something to say about who wins this year."

Hammersmith raised slightly bushy eyebrows. "Oh?" He turned away from Felicity, although with some visible reluctance, and faced Sam as he went on, "You're one of my competitors this year? You're new, aren't you?"

"Yep, first time," Sam said as he pumped

Hammersmith's hand. "Name's Sam Fletcher. Good to meet you, Jody."

"It's Joe D. First name and initial."

"Oh. I got you now."

Phyllis suspected that Sam had known all along what Hammersmith's name actually was. The so-called mistake was just a subtle dig at the man. Phyllis felt an instinctive dislike for Hammersmith and wouldn't be surprised if Sam did, too.

Hammersmith lost interest in Sam and turned back to Felicity, practically purring as he said, "I don't believe I caught your name, my dear."

"I'm Felicity Prosper. I'm sure you've seen me on *Inside Beat.*"

"You know, I believe I have." Phyllis figured Hammersmith would say that whether it was true or not. The man went on, "Wonderful show, just wonderful. And you do a spectacular job, Felicity. You don't mind if I call you Felicity, do you? I'm sure you'd like to do an interview with me."

"Well, I *had* planned on interviewing you, since you're the champion —"

"Well, why not right now?" Hammersmith interrupted her. Smoothly, he linked his arm with hers and turned her away from the others. "I know a nice quiet place where we can get a drink and talk about whatever you'd like. Just don't ask me to divulge my secret recipe!"

They both laughed at that, then Felicity said, "But you must be a little shaken up after that trouble —"

"Trouble?" Hammersmith waved his free hand in dismissal. "That was no trouble! Just a little misunderstanding. I'm fine."

"If I'm going to interview you, I should get my cameraman —"

"Let's just consider this a preliminary interview," Hammersmith said as he urged her along the line of recreational vehicles. "You know, we'll just lay out the ground-work."

Phyllis heard Josh mutter under his breath, "The groundwork's not all he wants to —"

Sam put a hand on the young man's shoulder as Hammersmith led Felicity away. "I don't reckon you have to worry, son," he said. "If there's anybody who can take care of herself, I think it's Ms. Prosper."

"Yeah, you're right about that," Josh agreed, nodding. "I don't know, though . . . You get two egos like that together, some-thing's liable to blow up."

"If it does, I'm sure we'll hear about it," Phyllis said. "Not to change the subject, but I'm a little surprised your boss sent Felicity to cover something like a chili cook-off.

Doesn't she usually do stories that are more . . ."

"Lurid?" Josh said. "Like violent crimes that have some sex angle?" His beefy shoulders rose and fell. "Yeah, I suppose so. But stories like those don't come along every week, you know. And since Felicity's getting paid a pretty good salary, the executive producer likes to keep her working as much as possible. So we get some human interest stories like this one. Anyway, this Hammersmith angle could be a good one. She can play up the guy as some sort of chili cook-off Casanova."

Eve laughed and said, "No offense, Josh, but I'm surprised someone as young as you knows who that was."

"Yes, ma'am. I'm an associate producer. It's my job to know things. Like, where are you folks headed now?"

"We're just takin' a walk and a look around," Sam said. "You want to come along?"

"Sure. Maybe we'll come across something else Felicity can do a report on."

Phyllis didn't see Felicity and Hammersmith anymore. She wondered if that "nice, quiet place where they could get a drink" was actually Hammersmith's motor home or travel trailer. But as Sam had said,

Felicity could take care of herself. A woman as attractive as she was probably had dealt with quite a few lecherous interview subjects over the course of her career.

The smell of food cooking filled the evening air. Chili dominated, as would be expected, given the setting, but Phyllis also smelled barbecue, steaks, fish, and an assortment of other enticing aromas. There was a faint undertone of exhaust fumes from the many generators in use, but the more pleasant smells kept it at bay.

The smell of food cooking wasn't the only thing in the air. Phyllis heard music coming from several different directions in the sprawling encampment, and as they walked past a large black motor home with silver lightning bolts painted on it, a fast-paced tune burst out from much closer. Sam clapped lightly in time with the music and said, " 'Foggy Mountain Breakdown'. One of my favorites."

"I think it's coming from right behind this motor home," Phyllis said. "Do you want to go watch?"

Sam pointed to stylized lettering on the side of the motor home that read *B.J. SAWYER AND THE LAVACA RIVER BAND.* "I never heard of those fellas before, but they're pretty good," he said. "Let's go have a look."

They walked through the lane between the motor home and a travel trailer and came in sight of a half-circle of about thirty spectators who were clapping along as four musicians played. Two guitars, a fiddle, and a bass finished the famous bluegrass tune and launched into another one.

In an open area between the band and the spectators, a lean, leathery man with long white hair and a bristling white beard danced a jig of sorts. He wore laced-up work boots, blue jean shorts that came down to just above his bony knees, and a black t-shirt with the logo of a heavy metal band on it. A camo cap was pulled down on his wild thatch of hair. He wore sunglasses even though night had just about finished settling down over the valley. A couple of floodlights mounted on the back of the motor home illuminated the scene.

The old-timer's scrawny legs flashed back and forth as he danced to the music. His arms pumped up and down. Phyllis couldn't help but laugh a little at his enthusiasm. Eve said, "My, he's certainly having a good time, isn't he?"

"He's got the rhythm, all right," Sam said with a grin. "Could be there's a mite of alcohol or other chemical enhancement involved."

"Or maybe he just likes to dance," Phyllis said. "Either way, he's putting on quite a show."

The crowd's clapping increased and whoops of encouragement rang out from some of the people who had gathered to watch. The white-bearded man didn't need much urging. The musicians, all of them wearing boots, jeans, and cowboy shirts, grinned at each other and picked up the pace even more, as if they were challenging the old-timer to keep up with them.

He rose to the occasion, matching his gyrating movements to the music. The song built to its crescendo and then stopped, and this time the musicians didn't start another one. The crowd was still clapping and cheering as the old man spun around a couple more times, then stopped and raised his arms in acknowledgment of the acclaim.

Then, as alarmed shouts replaced the cheers, he collapsed.

CHAPTER 4

Phyllis gasped at the unexpected sight. Eve said, "Oh, dear!" and Josh exclaimed, "Whoa!" Sam hurried forward to help.

The musicians were closer and reached the old-timer first. Before they could do anything to help him, however, he sat up, waved them away, and said, "I'm fine, dadgum it, I'm fine! Just got a little winded."

As if to prove it, he scrambled spryly back to his feet and grinned around at the worried crowd.

"See? Good as new!" he declared. "Come on, boys, play another one. I'm just gettin' started!"

"Maybe so, Mr. Boudreau, but we're a little tired," one of the guitar players said. "It was a long drive to get here all the way from Hallettsville today."

"I know, I know. Well, you boys rest up, then. You need to be good an' fresh for the big show tomorrow night. Anyway, I reckon

I ain't as young as I used to be."

The man took off his camo-patterned cap and swatted at his legs with it, knocking some of the dust off his shorts that had gotten on there from his spill. Sam stepped up to him and said, "You're Hiram Boudreau?"

The man turned and gave Sam the once-over through his dark glasses, then said, "That's me, sonny." Phyllis doubted that Boudreau was actually much older than Sam, if any. "Owner, mayor, and grand high poobah of Cactus Bluff. Have we met?"

"No, sir." Sam put out his hand. "I'm Sam Fletcher. I'm one of the competitors in the chili cook-off."

Boudreau grabbed his hand. "Welcome, welcome! Good to see you, son, and I wish you the best of luck. Wouldn't be no contest without fellas like you, and without the contest there might not be a Cactus Bluff. Hope you enjoy your stay." He glanced at the others. "These your friends?"

"That's right." Sam performed the introductions, then added, "Phyllis is gonna write an article about the cook-off for *A Taste of Texas* magazine."

"Well, how about that. A member of the media." Boudreau wrung Phyllis's hand for a second time. "I'm mighty glad to hear that, Miz Newsom. Hope you'll tell ever'body that Cactus Bluff is a little bit o' heaven on earth, all the way out here in West Texas."

"I think my editor would prefer that I write more about the chili and all the other food that people will be cooking this weekend, but I have to admit, from what I've seen of it so far Cactus Bluff does have a certain charm."

"It's a great place for folks to retire. Beautiful weather all year 'round, nothin' but peace and quiet as far as the eye can see . . . Yes, ma'am, folks'll never find a better spot to settle in and enjoy their golden years. If there's one thing we got plenty of, it's room!"

Josh said, "I'm a journalist, too, Mr. Boudreau. Josh Green, producer for *Inside Beat*. I'm sure you've seen our show —"

"Can't say as I have, son," Boudreau cut him off and turned to Eve. He clasped both of her hands in his and went on, "And what's your special talent, darlin', other than bein' downright lovely?"

"I'd be glad to tell you all about it," Eve said with a smile, "but you've already collapsed once this evening and I'm not sure your heart could take it."

Boudreau stared at her for a second, then threw back his head and let out a bray of laughter. "You, I like!" he said. "I want you to be my special guest at the show tomorrow night. In fact, all of you can be my guests. You'll have the best seats that way."

"We're obliged to you, Mr. Boudreau —" Sam began.

"Call me Hiram. Ever'body does."

"Thanks, Hiram," Josh said. "We appreciate —"

Boudreau gave him a chilly stare. "You got your press credentials, boy?"

"Well, yeah, but —"

"There'll be an area set aside for you, then."

Phyllis said, "It didn't occur to me that I might need press credentials. I'm still a little new at this, I guess."

Boudreau waved a hand and said, "Aw, no, don't worry about that. You folks'll still be my guest. You're my kinda people, I can tell it."

"Everybody sure is friendly here," Sam said. "First that Carson girl, and now you, Hiram."

"You mean McKayla?" Boudreau asked with a hint of sharpness in his voice.

"Yeah, I think that was her name."

"Wouldn't think to look at the gal that she's only sixteen, would you?"

"Sixteen?" Carolyn said. "I thought she

had to be twenty-two, at least."

"Nope. I'm thinkin' I might ought to make a sign to hang around her neck, just to be sure some o' these ol' boys around town this weekend behave themselves. Her daddy ain't the sort of fella you want to get on the wrong side of."

"Speaking of men behaving themselves," Phyllis said, "we met Mr. Hammersmith a little while ago. There seemed to be some sort of trouble between him and a man named Kurt . . ."

Boudreau nodded. "Kurt Middleton. He's been nursin' a grudge against ol' Joe D. for a while now. Claims it's because there used to be some sort o' hanky-panky goin' on between his wife Lindy and Joe D., but if you ask me, I figure the real reason is because Joe D. keeps beatin' him in the cook-off. Kurt sets as much store by his chili as he does his wife, I'd say."

Josh said, "But is Mr. Hammersmith, you know, trustworthy? I only ask because he, uh, went off for an interview with the reporter I work with —"

"Pretty gal?"

"Excuse me?"

"This reporter, she's a pretty gal?"

"Oh, yeah," Josh said. "She's beautiful." Then he looked embarrassed. Phyllis tried not to smile. It appeared that Josh still had quite a crush on Felicity Prosper, despite the fact that she seldom seemed to know he was around unless she needed him to do something for her.

"Well, that's no surprise," Boudreau said. "Joe D.'s got an eye for a good-lookin' woman, no doubt about that. But deep down, he's a good sort. You don't have to worry about your friend, son."

"I'm glad to hear that."

Boudreau looked around. The crowd had broken up after the musicians had gone back into the motor home they used as a tour bus. He said, "Reckon I'd best mosey on. I was just takin' a look around, makin' sure everything's goin' all right so far, you know. I got to keep on top o' things, me bein' the grand high poobah and all. I'm sure I'll see all you folks later." He gave Eve a wicked grin. "Especially you, darlin'. I want to hear more about whatever it is you think this ol' ticker o' mine couldn't take."

"I'm sure that can be arranged," Eve said.

Boudreau waved and wandered off into the throng of people walking around the encampment, headed to or from town, which was now brightly lit, an oasis of illumination in the vast desert of darkness that was West Texas.

"He's certainly a . . . colorful . . . character," Carolyn said with a note of disapproval in her voice. The number of things Carolyn disapproved of was legion, and it grew all the time. Phyllis knew she usually didn't really mean anything by it, though.

Sam said, "You'd have to be a little on the eccentric side to buy a whole town, especially if it was the next thing to a ghost town like Cactus Bluff was before Hiram came along."

"He owns the *whole* town?" Phyllis said.

"That's what I've heard."

Eve said in a speculative tone, "He must be very wealthy, if he owns a town."

Carolyn gave her a look. Eve had been married several times, usually to men with money, and most of the matches had not worked out well. After the last one had ended tragically, Eve had sworn off marriage, but it appeared that determination might be wearing off.

Phyllis noted that and suggested, "Why don't we see what else there is to see?" Carolyn needed to be distracted before she made some caustic comment.

They walked on toward town, and as they did, they passed numerous spaces where people had set up propane-fueled grills outside motor homes and travel trailers.

Some, Phyllis noticed, were using charcoal or wood chips for burning. Sam's set-up used propane. Phyllis loved the taste of wood-smoked meat, but that didn't really apply when it came to chili. A steady, well-regulated heat was more important.

Sam stopped to talk to some of the people who were cooking. The conversations were pleasant enough but definitely guarded, which came as no surprise to Phyllis. She and Carolyn had been good friends for decades, but when they had been competing against each other in baking contests, they had always played their recipe cards very close to the vest, despite that friendship.

They reached the big tent, which was open on the sides. Nothing was going on in there tonight, so it was empty, but enough light penetrated into it from town and from the generator-powered lamps burning in the encampment for Phyllis to make out a number of tables set up at one end. At the other end was a raised stage where the musical acts would perform. Right in front of the stage was an open area, no doubt for dancing, and then rows of folding chairs where people could sit and watch and listen to the performances.

A smaller tent to one side had its side

walls lowered. A sign over the door read OFFICE. McKayla Carson stood in front of it, talking to an older man who was tall, burly, and mostly bald. He didn't look happy and kept shaking his head. Hiram Boudreau had mentioned McKayla's father, and Phyllis wondered if that was who the man was. Then she and her companions had moved on past the office tent without either McKayla or the man she was talking to seeming to notice them.

A similar tent had a sign on it that read SECURITY. A tall, brown-haired young man in brown uniform pants and tan uniform shirt stood there listening to a voice crackling over a walkie-talkie. After a moment the voice stopped and the officer keyed the microphone to say, "All right, Ken, if it starts to look like you can't handle it, let me know and I'll be right there."

"Trouble, Deputy?" Josh asked, evidently on the look-out for a possible story.

"It's Constable," the uniformed man replied as he lowered the walkie-talkie. Phyllis noted that he had a Taser clipped to his belt but wasn't carrying a gun as far as she could see. He went on, "And no offense, sir, but that's not really any of your business."

"I'm not a civilian," Josh said. "I'm a

member of the press. Josh Green, associate producer of *Inside Beat*."

The constable didn't appear to be impressed. "Just move along, folks," he said. "Enjoy your stay in Cactus Bluff. There's nothing to be concerned about."

The walkie-talkie crackled again, and this time Phyllis could make out the words as the man on the other end said in an excited voice, "Chuck, you better get over here! Looks like there's gonna be a fight, and it could turn into a real brawl!"

The constable made a face and lifted the walkie-talkie to his mouth. "On my way, Ken," he snapped. Then he hurried over to the Jeep Phyllis had noticed earlier, which was now parked beside the Security tent, and got in. Gravel rasped and flew under the tires as the constable backed up, turned, and headed for Cactus Bluff's small downtown area.

"I wonder what that was about," Josh said as he looked after the vehicle.

"There's already a bunch of folks here, even though there'll be more comin' in tomorrow," Sam said. "Put a crowd together, throw in enough high spirits and booze, and there's bound to be a few scrapes. I suspect that's all that's goin' on."

"I ought to check it out anyway. It's my

duty as a newsman. I just wish I knew where Nick got off to. Felicity gave him the evening off, since we weren't expecting to do any interviews until tomorrow."

"He has a cell phone, doesn't he?" Carolyn said. "Why don't you just call him?"

Josh looked dubious and said, "Nick doesn't like to be disturbed when he's not supposed to be working. I mean, sure, I'd call him if it was an emergency. I am the producer, after all. Well, associate producer. But technically, I *am* his boss . . ."

"We're headin' toward town anyway," Sam said as he clapped a hand on Josh's shoulder. "If we see something that looks like a big story, you can call him then. If it doesn't amount to anything, then you won't have disturbed him for no reason."

"Yeah, that'll work," Josh said. The eagerness with which he accepted the suggestion told Phyllis he was grateful to Sam for helping him save face. The five of them started on toward town, following the same gravel road the constable had taken in his Jeep.

As night had fallen, a number of booths selling food and souvenirs had opened up along the side of the paved road at the edge of town. It reminded Phyllis of a carnival as she saw people hawking popcorn, cotton candy, nachos, and hot dogs. At one booth the owner was spinning up funnel cakes. Eve pointed to it and said, "I'll bet those aren't nearly as good as the ones you used to make, Phyllis."

"Probably not," Carolyn agreed, "but I suspect Phyllis doesn't have very good memories of those funnel cakes she made for the State Fair a few years ago."

The incident Carolyn referred to was yet another instance when murder had reared its ugly head in an unlikely place. Phyllis didn't try to block the affair from her mind or anything like that, but she didn't like to dwell on it, either.

To lighten the mood, she said, "It's been a while since I made any funnel cakes. Maybe I'll do that when we get home."

"Funnel cakes sound good," Josh said. "I might stop and get some of those on the way back. Right now I want to find out why that guy had to call in the constable. Who do you think he was? Do they have deputy constables?"

"We'll find out," Sam said. He pointed along the street toward an old-fashioned rock building with a red slate roof. The constable's Jeep was parked beside it, along with quite a few other cars, pickups, and SUVs. "Looks like a beer joint."

They walked past the other booths. Phyllis saw cheap Indian jewelry for sale, along with rugs, paintings on velvet, and what were probably bootleg DVDs and computer games.

As they approached their destination, the tavern's front door flew open and several men spilled through it, tangled up in a fistfight. Punches flew back and forth, most of them missing. Some of the men began wrestling and wound up on the ground, rolling around. Phyllis and the others stopped in their tracks to watch the brawl. She didn't see the constable anywhere and wondered where he was.

Then another figure rushed out the door, this one wearing high heels, tight jeans, and a silk blouse. She jumped on the back of one of the combatants, locked an arm around the man's neck, and started punching at him with her other hand.

"Holy cow!" Josh yelled. "That's Felicity!"

CHAPTER 5

Josh ran toward the fighters. Sam would have started after him, but Phyllis caught hold of his arm and said, "Sam, you're too old to get mixed up in a bar brawl."

Sam looked torn. Phyllis believed he knew she was right, but at the same time he wanted to pitch in and help Josh. He confirmed that by saying, "I don't want that kid to get hurt."

"He won't be," Phyllis said. "Here comes the law."

The constable charged out of the tavern, followed by another uniformed officer. The constable was bleeding from a cut on his forehead, but that didn't seem to slow him down any as he grabbed a couple of the fighters and shoved them apart. The other officer, a heavyset older man with close-cropped salt-and-pepper hair, did likewise, wading into the brawl and breaking it up as best he could.

The man whose back Felicity had jumped onto was spinning around, trying to dislodge her. He succeeded just as Josh reached them. Felicity let out a cry of alarm as she lost her grip and flew backward. Josh was there to catch her, but the collision knocked him backward and made him lose his balance. He fell over, landing on his back with Felicity sprawled on top of him. His arms were around her, and he didn't seem to be in any hurry to let her go.

"Break it up, break it up!" the constable shouted. "I'm going to arrest all of you if you don't stop it!"

Eve tugged on Phyllis's sleeve and said, "There's that man Hammersmith."

It was true. Joe D. Hammersmith was lying on the ground, looking slightly dazed. Phyllis realized that the man Felicity had attacked was the one who knocked Hammersmith down a second before the TV personality jumped on his back. Hammersmith must have made a good impression on Felicity for her to come to his defense like that.

The lawmen were succeeding in stopping the fight. They were aided by other patrons of the bar who had come out to grab their friends and hold them back. The constable raised his hands and said, "Everybody just settle down, blast it!"

Hiram Boudreau appeared, no doubt drawn by the commotion, and asked the constable, "What happened here, Chuck?"

"I haven't had a chance to get all the details yet," Chuck replied, "but you know how these things get started, Mayor. Somebody takes offense at something — it doesn't really matter what — and then throws a punch, and drinks get spilled, and before you know it everybody's trying to beat up everybody else."

"Well, you'll see to it that order's restored, right?"

"It just about is." Chuck looked around with a grim expression on his blood-streaked face. "I just have to figure out who's going to jail."

Boudreau's hands fluttered as he made little patting motions. "Oh, now, we don't have to throw anybody in jail, do we? You know things get a mite high-spirited durin' the cook-off, but I'm sure none o' these fellas meant any real harm."

Phyllis understood Boudreau's reaction. A bunch of arrests would be bad for the cook-off's reputation. Bad for business. Chuck frowned, though, and looked like he wasn't disposed toward letting the troublemakers off the hook.

Felicity distracted everyone from that confrontation by yelping, "Damn it, Josh, let me up!"

Josh was still lying on his back where he had fallen, like an overturned turtle. Only it was Felicity's arms and legs that waved in the air, not his. He let go of her and she rolled off of him, then struggled to her feet and furiously brushed off her jeans. Her expression said that she was trying to maintain at least a shred of dignity, but it wasn't easy.

Joe D. Hammersmith had made it to hands and knees. Felicity stepped over and took his arm to help him up. He had a bruise forming on his jaw where he'd been punched, but that didn't stop him from grinning as he said, "You leaped into the fray like a valkyrie, my dear!"

Felicity still looked disgusted. "Yeah, well, if the defending champion can't cook because he's in the hospital, the story's not as good. Why did that guy come over and attack you like that, anyway? That started the whole thing!"

The constable said, "I'd like to hear the answer to that, too."

The man Felicity had jumped on pointed a finger at Hammersmith and said in a loud, angry voice, "I'll tell you why I went after this skunk! He's a no-good card cheat! He took eight hundred dollars off me in a crooked poker game at last year's cook-off. I told him earlier that he'd better pay up, and if he didn't, the next time I saw him we were goin' to Fist City! He didn't pay, so I figured I'd take it out of his hide."

"That's a lie," Hammersmith said as he scowled at the man. "A damnable lie. You're just a sore loser, Porter, and that's all it amounts to."

Porter clenched his fists and started to take a step toward Hammersmith, but the constable moved between them.

"So this fight started over a gambling debt?" Chuck said.

"No debt," Hammersmith said with a sneer. "I beat him fair and square. Just like my Hammersmith Deluxe beats his watery, pathetic excuse for chili year after year."

This time the other officer had to grab Porter from behind to hold him back. Evidently insulting a man's chili was worse than winning hundreds of dollars from him in a poker game, Phyllis thought.

"So Porter went after you, and the fight spread from there?" Chuck said to Hammersmith.

"That's right. Lock him up, Constable. I want him charged with assault!"

"Hold on, hold on," Boudreau said quickly. "If Porter's behind bars, he can't take part in the cook-off. We need a full field o' chili cooks, Chuck." He turned to Hammersmith. "Surely you understand that better'n anybody else, Joe D."

"He's afraid of me," Porter ranted before Hammersmith could say anything. "He's scared I'll beat him this year! That's why he wants me locked up!"

Hammersmith's jaw jutted out defiantly. "Afraid of you and that swill you call chili? Ha!" He flapped a hand. "Forget it. I'm not pressing charges. And I'm not giving back that eight hundred dollars I won fair and square."

Chuck said, "I could arrest all of you for disturbing the peace whether anybody presses charges or not." He pointed to the cut on his forehead. "That's all the evidence I need, right there."

"No need to be hasty —" Boudreau began.

Chuck blew out a disgusted breath. "All right, all right. We'll forget the whole thing . . . this time. You should get the word around, though, Mayor, that everything had better stay peaceful for the rest of the weekend. I don't want any more of these ruckuses!"

"You betcha," Boudreau answered without

hesitation. He looked at the other officer. "We'll see to it, won't we, Ken?"

"Sure, boss," the man said. Phyllis could see now that the uniform he wore was that of a hired security company, not the sheriff's department or the state troopers. He turned to the crowd, waved his arms, and went on, "Break it up, break it up! Fun's over! Everybody go on about your business!"

Chuck turned to Hammersmith and asked, "Is anybody else nursing a grudge against you?"

"Certainly not. As the perennial champion, I'm a beloved figure at these get-togethers. Of course, I can't rule out jealousy on the part of the losers who go down to defeat every year."

Chuck just snorted at that and turned away.

Sam put a hand on Josh's shoulder and asked, "You all right, son?"

"Yeah, I . . . I'm fine. It's Felicity I'm worried about."

"Don't worry about me," she snapped. "I'm not hurt." Grudgingly, she added, "Thanks for being there to break my fall, I guess."

Josh's face lit up like the sun. "Oh, gee, I . . . I'm just glad I could help —"

"But don't think I didn't notice that you

were trying to cop a feel while you were at it."

His eyes widened and his face turned red. "What? I never —"

Felicity turned away dismissively and asked Hammersmith, "So, do you get in fights like this all the time?"

Sam drawled, "Second one tonight."

Hammersmith glared at him for a second, then said, "Both misunderstandings, I assure you."

"I'm afraid I don't buy that about you being a beloved figure," Felicity said. "Nobody likes someone who wins all the time."

"I just do my best," Hammersmith said with what struck Phyllis as false modesty. "It's the judges who decide who wins."

"I suppose. I'll still want to get an on-camera interview with you."

Hammersmith nodded toward the tavern. "We can go back in and discuss it over some more drinks. There won't be any more trouble."

"No, that's all right. I'll find you in the morning and we'll set something up. It's been a long day."

"You're sure?" Hammersmith was nothing if not persistent.

Josh spoke up. "The lady said no."

"I don't need you to act chivalrous,"

Felicity said. "Let's go."

She started off toward the encampment. Josh hurried after her.

Carolyn scowled after them and said, "She treats that young man shamefully."

"And yet he still looks at her as if she were the sun, the moon, and the stars all wrapped up in one package," Eve said. "There's no fathoming the mystery of the human heart."

Carolyn snorted. "Spoken like an English teacher. He's not thinking with his heart."

Phyllis said, "You might be surprised."

She looked around and saw something that took *her* slightly by surprise. McKayla Carson had come up and was using a handkerchief to try to wipe some of the blood off Constable Chuck's face. She was standing pretty close to him while she did that, and the young lawman looked a little uncomfortable. He probably knew that she was underage, as Boudreau had mentioned earlier. But he didn't take the handkerchief and put some distance between them, Phyllis noticed. She looked around and saw no sign of the balding older man who had been talking to McKayla earlier.

Now that the fight was over, they moved on up the street, along with the hundreds of other people who were in Cactus Bluff tonight. Now that she had a better chance to look around, Phyllis saw that in addition to Boudreau's Market and the Boudreau Hotel, the town's businesses also included Boudreau's Café, Boudreau's Farm and Ranch Supply, Boudreau's Propane and Propane Accessories, Boudreau's Garage, and the Cactus Bluff *Star*, Hiram Boudreau, Publisher.

"He really does own the whole town, doesn't he?" she said.

"Appears he does," Sam said.

"Where did he get his money?"

"Couldn't tell you. I never looked the fella up, except for the little bit they've got about him on the website where you sign up for the chili cook-off." Sam pointed to Boudreau's Café. "Why don't we go in there and see if they've got any pie left?"

"We already ate supper," Carolyn pointed out.

"Yeah, but that was hours ago. A piece of pie in the evening doesn't really count, anyway."

Phyllis smiled and said, "How do you figure that?"

"Well, if it's fruit pie, then it's healthy, right?"

"We've had this discussion before. You're not going to win it."

"I don't care about winnin', as long as I

get pie."

Carolyn said, "Well, I'm not going to eat anything this late, because I won't sleep well if I do. And I'm sure they don't have anything gluten-free. But don't let that stop you."

They went into the café, which was busy even though the supper rush was over by now. The tables had old-fashioned red-and-white-checked tablecloths on them, and they were all occupied except for a couple. Sam pointed to one of the empty tables and led the way across the crowded room, past the counter where more customers sat on stools with red naugahyde seats. Phyllis thought the place would have looked pretty much the same if they had walked in here in 1957. The intervening sixty years hadn't caught up to Cactus Bluff in some ways.

They sat down and a harried-looking waitress in a light blue uniform came over to them. "The kitchen's about to close, folks," she said, "but I can go check and see what's left if you want."

"How about pie?" Sam asked.

"Oh, yeah, sure, we have buttermilk and apple."

"I'll take a slice of the buttermilk."

"You got it. Ladies?"

Carolyn said, "Nothing for me, thanks."

Phyllis looked at Eve and asked, "Would you like to split a slice of apple pie?"

"That sounds like a good idea," Eve agreed.

The waitress managed a smile and a nod. "I'll be right back with it. How about some coffee? There's regular and decaf if you want it."

They shook their heads to that offer. The waitress went off to fetch the pie. Phyllis said to Sam, "I thought you were going to get fruit pie because it's healthy."

"Yeah, but I *really* like buttermilk pie. And since it's made with buttermilk, it counts as dairy . . . right?"

While they waited, Carolyn said, "That Hammersmith man seems like he's trouble. He fools around with other men's wives, he cheats at cards, he wins every year . . . There's no telling what else he does to make people angry at him."

A man sitting at the table next to him turned his chair halfway around and looked over his shoulder. "Excuse me for buttin' in," he said. "Did I just hear you talking about Joe D. Hammersmith?"

"That's right," Phyllis said warily. "Is he a friend of yours?"

"A friend?" the man repeated. "Joe D.

Hammersmith can go straight to hell as far as I'm concerned, the no-good chili cheat!"

CHAPTER 6

The man tipped back the cap he wore and went on, "Sorry if he's a friend of yours, but I just can't stand the no-good —"

The woman sitting at the table with him reached over, put a hand on his arm, and said, "You don't need to be getting so upset, Roger. Remember what the doctor said about your blood pressure and stress."

"Yeah, yeah," the man muttered. "I just can't stand that Hammersmith." He looked at Phyllis and the others. "No offense."

"We just met the fella this evenin', so you're not offendin' us," Sam assured him. "I do seem to remember seein' his name on the cook-off's website, but that's all I ever knew about him until today."

"And none of the rest of us had even heard of him," Phyllis added.

"But from what we've seen of him," Carolyn put in, "he's not the sort of man we'd ever be friends with."

The man turned his chair halfway around so he could see them better and nodded. "I'm not sure he's got any real friends except maybe Hiram Boudreau, and Hiram just likes him because he's turned into the star of the cook-off and that gets publicity." He stuck his hand out to Sam. "Name's Roger Glennister. This is my wife Julie."

Julie Glennister, a pleasant-looking woman with fluffy blond hair, smiled and nodded while Sam and her husband shook hands. "Hello, folks," she said. "Which one of you is the chili cook? Or are you all entering the contest?"

"That'd be me," Sam said. "Although Carolyn here is gonna enter a couple of the side contests." He introduced the others, and more pleasantries were exchanged.

Glennister took his cap off, revealing thinning brown hair. Even though he was dressed in jeans and a khaki shirt and had a cap with a farm implement logo on it, Phyllis thought he looked more like an insurance salesman than a farmer. Of course, there was no reason he couldn't have an insurance agency *and* a farm. And those were just wild guesses, so she could be totally wrong about him.

"Where are you from?" Glennister asked. "Julie and I are in Granbury."

"Well, you're not very far from us, then," Sam said. "All of us live in Weatherford."

"Is that so?" Glennister reached into the pocket of his work shirt. "Let me give you a card. I have clients in Weatherford, and I'm always glad to add another."

Phyllis caught a glimpse of the logo on the card and saw that she'd been right. Glennister was an agent for a large insurance company.

"So tell me about your chili," he went on as he handed the card to Sam.

"It's really good," Sam said. "How about yours?"

Glennister laughed. "Not giving away any secrets, are you?"

Sam grinned and said, "Nope."

"Well, mine's really good, too, and that's enough said about that, I suppose. We'll find out in a couple of days, won't we?"

Phyllis said, "I'm curious about something. You called Joe D. Hammersmith a chili cheat. How in the world do you go about cheating when it comes to cooking chili?"

Glennister put his cap back on, pulled it down tight, scowled, and said, "He's a precooker."

"No," Sam said as his eyes widened.

"Excuse me," Eve said. "What am I missing here?"

Sam turned to her and explained, "You're not allowed to use any pre-cooked ingredients other than tomato sauce or other commercial stuff like that. Any fresh ingredients have to be cooked in the pot, especially the meat." He looked at Glennister again. "Are you sayin' he pre-cooks his meat?"

"I know good and well he does." Glennister shrugged. "It's just that nobody's been able to catch him at it and prove it. The guy can do sleight-of-hand like a dang magician."

With a solemn expression on his face, Sam shook his head slowly. "That's just not right."

"Why not?" Carolyn asked. "I'm sorry, but I don't see how it could make that much difference."

Phyllis said, "I imagine it has to do with being able to make sure the meat you're using is tender and spiced just the way you want it."

"That's right," Sam said. "Sometimes you might need more cookin' time than what you're allowed. Or you might have some meat where the taste doesn't turn out exactly like you want it. If you pre-cook, you can throw out anything that's not perfect and start over until the taste is just right. Then you slip that meat into your chili and nobody knows the difference. It sort of takes the human element out of things. Every cook can foul up a recipe now and then."

Carolyn gave an eloquent little sniff that said plainly she didn't believe *she* would ever do such a thing.

Phyllis said, "So this pre-cooking would be a major rules violation, something bad enough for Hammersmith to be disqualified if he was caught at it?"

"That's right," Glennister said. "The trick is catching him at it. So far nobody's been able to do that. But a lot of us have our suspicions."

But without proof, Phyllis thought, that was all they were — suspicions. She wondered if jealousy and frustration caused by Hammersmith's continued success had anything to do with what the other contestants suspected.

The waitress brought the slices of pie over to the table. Glennister and his wife had finished what appeared to be a late supper, so they stood up and Glennister picked up the check from the table. He shook hands with Sam again and said, "See you tomorrow. Good luck to you."

"Same to you," Sam said.

"Good night, ladies," Julie told Phyllis, Carolyn, and Eve. They returned the sentiment, and the Glennisters left the café.

"Nice folks," Sam said.

"They seem to be," Phyllis agreed.

They ate their pie, which in Phyllis's opinion was quite good. The place was clearing out some now, although the street, as seen through the front window and framed by homey curtains, was still fairly busy with pedestrians and slow-moving vehicle traffic. When the pie was gone, Sam paid the bill, refusing offers from Phyllis and Eve to cover the piece they had split, and the four of them started walking back toward the encampment.

This time they didn't run into any trouble along the way. When they reached the large gravel lot where Sam's pickup was parked, Phyllis told him, "You don't have to walk us all the way back to the travel trailer."

"That's all right," he said. "I'd rather see that you ladies are safe for the night in the War Wagon before I turn in. Besides, we spent enough time sittin' today that stretchin' my legs still feels good."

"Well, I don't mind the company," Phyllis said with a smile.

When they reached the travel trailer, Carolyn said, "I'm exhausted, and I need to be up early in the morning to see about entering those other contests. You're sure I didn't need to sign up for them ahead of time, Sam?"

"Nope. The actual chili cook-off is the only thing where you have to get your entry in early if you want to have a place."

"I'm going to go to bed, then," Carolyn said. "Good night."

"I'll turn in, too," Eve announced. "Although I might work a little first."

"Are you writin' another book?" Sam asked. A while back, Eve had written a mystery novel loosely based on the four of them, and she had not only sold it to a publisher, but a film production company had bought the rights to it as well. So far nothing had come of that, but Eve had cautioned them that the wheels in Hollywood ground exceedingly slow.

"I've started another one," Eve said, "but I haven't gotten much done so far. I thought it might help jump-start the movie deal if I had another book out. Of course, if it's a failure that will probably kill the whole thing."

"It won't be a failure," Phyllis said. "I'm confident of that. Your first book was excellent."

"We'll see." Eve lifted a hand and added,

"Good night, you two," then stepped up into the trailer.

Phyllis turned to Sam. He rested his hands lightly on her shoulders, leaned forward, kissed her on the forehead, and then they embraced for a moment. They were more than friends, but neither was comfortable with public displays of affection — and with all the people still wandering around, this was certainly a public place.

"See you in the mornin'," Sam said. "Hope you sleep well."

"You, too." She squeezed his arm and they exchanged a smile, then Sam turned and strolled back toward the parking area and his pickup.

She watched him go for a moment, then climbed into the travel trailer, smiling a little as she thought about how he had dubbed it the War Wagon. A small lamp was lit in the living area, but the rest of the trailer was dark and quiet. Eve must have decided not to try to write after all. She and Carolyn were sharing the queen-size bed that folded down in the rear section, where one of the pop-out sections was located. The other pop-out was toward the front, where the folding sofa bed was.

Phyllis left the sofa folded for the time being and took her laptop from the technology bag she had stashed with the rest of her things. She was tired but not particularly sleepy, so she had decided to give in to her curiosity and try to find out more about Hiram Boudreau, the mayor and "grand high poobah" of Cactus Bluff.

She sat on the sofa, opened the computer, and searched for a wireless network. BoudreauNetGuest popped up immediately. Having seen *Free WiFi* signs posted in many of the businesses, she had expected as much. The password, which came up on the log-in screen, was *Boudreau1*. Smiling, Phyllis entered it and logged in.

After checking her email and not finding anything urgent she needed to deal with, she searched for Hiram Boudreau's name and got several pages worth of hits. The first ones, which all came from various newspaper and TV station websites, had to do with the chili cook-off and showcased those media outlets' coverage of past events. She found the site Sam had used to sign up for the contest and scrolled on through to the second page of hits.

Several links down on this page was one that led to an article from a Midland newspaper. The headline read *A/B Exploration Sold*.

Phyllis clicked through to it and read the

story. According to the newspaper, an oil exploration and drilling company owned by Harlan Anders and Hiram Boudreau had been sold to one of the larger oil companies for an undisclosed price rumored to be in the low eight figures. So at least ten million dollars, Phyllis mused. Only the company hadn't been sold by both partners, she discovered, but rather by Hiram Boudreau, whose partner in the business, Harlan Anders, had succumbed to cancer six months earlier.

Boudreau and Anders had started the company in the early Eighties and seen it grow and succeed considerably in the more than thirty years since.

Boudreau was quoted in the newspaper as saying, "After Harlan passed away, the heart for the oil business sort of went out of me, you know? I never married and had children, but the company was sort of like my baby. It just wasn't the same with Harlan gone, though. You lose somebody close and it makes you think. So I decided it was time to sell and find something else to do with the time I've got left."

Phyllis checked the date on the newspaper story. Six and a half years earlier. She searched and found Harlan Anders' obituary, which also mentioned Boudreau. Anders had been a widower, but he had two adult children, a son and a daughter, both of whom lived in Midland. The photograph of Anders with the obituary showed a mild-looking, gray-haired man with glasses who reminded Phyllis more of a college professor than an oilfield wildcatter — if that was even what they were called anymore.

She scrolled through the rest of the hits, found a small story about Boudreau buying the mostly abandoned town of Cactus Bluff with plans for revitalizing and developing it. Phyllis wasn't sure how much revitalizing had gone on around here, except during the weekend of the chili cook-off, but that might be enough. All the other stories she found on various websites, blogs, and social media pages were about the contest itself. She was a little surprised to see how many people wrote about cooking chili, but she supposed she shouldn't have been. Any subject or activity had its aficionados, and the internet brought them all together.

There were even true crime websites that talked about her and the murders she had solved.

But it was her hope they wouldn't have anything new to write about for a long time, if ever, she thought as she got ready to fold out the sofa bed and turn in.

CHAPTER 7

Phyllis was never one to sleep too late. All those years of getting up and going to school had made her a fairly early riser. Carolyn was the same way, although Eve liked to sleep in. Phyllis had the coffee going in the travel trailer's small kitchen and dining area when Carolyn came in from the sleeping area in the back.

"I didn't think I'd sleep very well last night," Carolyn said as she sat down at the small table. "I usually don't in a strange bed. But I guess the trip yesterday made me so tired I went out like a light."

"The higher altitude and the cleaner air might have something to do with it, too," Phyllis said. She poured a cup of coffee and set it in front of her friend, the brew strong and black the way Carolyn liked it.

She went to the small refrigerator and opened it to get some eggs, in the process reaching around the packages of meat Sam had brought with him for the chili. He was making three batches using cubed tri-tip roast beef. The first one would be a test batch so Carolyn could use it for her leftover chili recipe. Phyllis had eaten Sam's chili and thought it was delicious. And that wasn't just because of her feelings for Sam. She didn't let friendship color her opinion of food.

She had scrambled eggs, bacon, and biscuits just about ready when a soft knock sounded on the door. Carolyn went over to open it and admit Sam into the trailer.

"Mornin', ladies," he greeted them, then paused and took a deep breath. "Smells mighty good, as usual."

"Help yourself to the coffee," Phyllis told him. "How did you sleep last night?"

"Just fine. This isn't the first time I've used that old air mattress and sleeping bag in the back of my pickup. I've slept out like that everywhere from Padre Island to the high lonesome in the Rockies."

"What's on the agenda for today?" Carolyn asked. "I need to sign up for those other contests, don't I?"

"Yeah, those'll start around the middle of the day tomorrow, from what I understand, just like the chili preliminaries. The finals for the chili cookin' are on Sunday and a big fireworks display on Sunday evenin' for Fourth of July. Then come Monday mornin', everybody'll be headin' out. It'll be a busy time until then."

"Will you be cooking the chili here?" Phyllis asked.

"Tomorrow, yeah. I'll set my grill up right outside, if that's all right with you, and will do a practice run today so Carolyn'll have some chili to work with for her leftover chili recipe. On Sunday all the cookin' will move into the tent for the finals. That's the big day for the spectators."

Carolyn shook her head. "I'm still not sure I understand how watching a bunch of people cook chili is a spectator sport. But then, I don't understand the appeal of watching men drive their cars around and around in a circle, either, and there seem to be millions of people who enjoy that."

Sam chuckled and said, "How can you call yourself a Texan if you're not a NASCAR fan?"

"I don't have a problem with that at all," Carolyn said.

The smell of the food cooking must have drifted to Eve and roused her from sleep. She came into the dining area wearing silk pajamas. Phyllis was already dressed in cropped jeans and a short-sleeved t-shirt, while Carolyn wore a simple sleeveless cotton dress that sported big pockets, in one of which she put her cell phone.

"I hope I didn't disturb you during the night," she said to Carolyn. "I know neither of us is used to sharing a bed these days."

"No, you didn't bother me," Carolyn assured her.

Eve veered toward the counter where the coffeemaker sat. She got a cup and was filling it when a loud boom suddenly came from somewhere outside. The explosion was loud enough that Phyllis thought she felt the trailer shiver a little under her feet.

"What the hell!" Sam yelled. That was a good indicator of how startled he was, because he seldom cursed. He was still standing, so he set the cup of coffee he was holding on the counter and then practically leaped to the door and threw it open. Phyllis was right behind him as he jumped to the ground, not bothering with the steps.

She stopped in the doorway and said, "Wait, Sam. You don't know what's going on. You shouldn't rush off into trouble."

"Something blew up, I know that much," he said. He lifted his arm and pointed. "Over there!"

Phyllis saw black smoke billowing up from somewhere a few rows away in the ranks of parked motor homes and travel trailers. All around the encampment, people were pouring out of their vehicles, running around aimlessly, shouting questions, and then starting toward the smoke when they spotted it. She knew Sam would be headed in that direction, too, so she hurried down the steps and joined him.

Somewhere in the distance, a siren began to blare. Phyllis could barely hear it over the hubbub that filled the air.

"What in the world happened?" she said.

"Something blowed up real good," Sam said. "I'll go see what it was."

"Not by yourself you won't," she told him. "And whatever it was, you'd better not get too close. Something else might explode."

"That's a good reason for you to stay here."

Phyllis wasn't going to waste time arguing with him. She took off toward the rising smoke. Sam's long legs allowed him to catch up easily, and after that they hurried along together, joining an ever-growing throng of people headed toward the apparent source of the explosion.

They cut through between vehicles parked along two rows and came out into an open area. On the next row, several spaces over, a long motor home was burning fiercely, throwing off what was now a thick column of black smoke that rose into the sky and angled north, carried in that direction by the early morning breeze from the south. A large crowd had already gathered to watch the conflagration.

The parking spaces were narrow enough that the vehicles on either side of the burning motor home were at risk from the blaze. To the left was another motor home, and as Phyllis and Sam watched, its owner — more than likely — climbed behind the wheel and shouted through an open window for everybody to get out of the way. He started the engine and eased forward, turning to get away from the burning motor home but having to go slowly because of all the people still blocking his path.

On the other side, a travel trailer was parked to the right of the fire. A man worked desperately to get it hitched to a pickup so it could be pulled out of danger, too. That was made more difficult by the fact that the heat given off by the blaze was so fierce no one could stand to get too close to it for very long. Phyllis could feel the heat even where she and Sam were standing, a considerable distance away.

The siren got louder. The constable's Jeep came into view. Bystanders scurried out of the way, but Chuck couldn't go very fast, either. He finally stopped when he was fairly close to the burning motor home and got out of the Jeep carrying a fire extinguisher. He ran toward the blaze, then stopped short and stared at the flames. Phyllis could tell by the sudden slump of his shoulders that he'd realized the little fire extinguisher wasn't going to do any good against something like this.

He turned, waved an arm, and shouted, "Get back! Everybody stay back!"

Phyllis said to Sam, "Do you think the gas tank has already exploded?"

"I believe it might have," he said with a frown. "I didn't really pay much attention when it happened because I was so surprised, but now that I think about it, seems like maybe there was more than one explosion. More like three, each one bigger than the last. But they were all so close together, it almost sounded like one blast."

Phyllis considered that idea for a moment and then nodded. "You could be right," she said. "You think something else blew up first and then took the gas tank with it."

"If that's what happened, I'd bet it was a propane tank that went up first."

That made sense to Phyllis. Most of these vehicles used propane tanks or cylinders in their kitchens to start with, and at a chili cook-off like this, there would be plenty of propane-fueled grills, too. She looked at the burning motor home and said, "If there was anybody in there . . ."

"They wouldn't have had a chance," Sam finished.

The constable had cleared all the bystanders back for a good distance. Hiram Boudreau came running up, bony red knees flying, skinny arms pumping, a floppy-brimmed straw hat on his head today but otherwise dressed much the same as he had been the day before.

"What happened?" he yelped. "What the hell happened?"

"I don't know," Chuck told him. "I just got here myself. Did you call the volunteer fire department?"

"Yeah, but you know as well as I do that it'll be forty-five minutes before the truck gets here!"

It was already too late to save anyone who had been near the explosion, Phyllis thought. The motor home would just have to burn itself out. The man who had been working to move the travel trailer next to it had finally succeeded in getting the trailer hooked up. With a roar from his pickup's engine, he pulled the trailer away. The sides of it looked a little scorched, but that appeared to be the extent of the damage.

Eve had gotten dressed, and now she and Carolyn joined Phyllis and Sam. Carolyn looked at the blaze and said, "Good heavens! Do you know if anyone was hurt?"

Phyllis shook her head. "We haven't heard anything yet. We don't know what caused the explosion or who that motor home belonged to.

Sam looked around and spotted a familiar face. He called, "Hey, Roger!"

Roger and Julie Glennister were standing about twenty feet away in the crowd. Roger lifted a hand in greeting at Sam's hail. Sam worked his way over to join the couple. Phyllis, Carolyn, and Eve followed.

"You know what happened?" Sam and Roger asked at the same time, then each of them shook his head.

"Sounded like a propane tank blew up," Roger said, "and it got the motor home's gas tank, too."

"That's just what we were sayin'," Sam agreed. "Any idea who owns that thing?"

Roger shook his head again. "Maybe if I could see it better, but shoot, the whole thing's just a big ball of fire."

"The poor people who were in it," Julie said. A shudder went through her. "I can't stand to even think about it."

"We don't know that anyone was in it," Phyllis said. She wasn't familiar enough with propane grills and tanks to know if it was possible that one could have blown up by itself, with no one around. *Something* would have to set off a spark . . .

Despite the futility of it, the constable began spraying foam from his fire extinguisher onto the blaze. Some of the spectators ran back to their motor homes and trailers and returned with extinguishers of their own. Soon more than a dozen people were spraying the flames, and after a couple of minutes the fierce conflagration began to subside.

"Looks like they're gonna get it put out," Sam said. "That'll keep the fire from spreadin', anyway."

Behind the group of people with fire extinguishers, Hiram Boudreau hopped back and forth from foot to foot like a little boy needing to go to the bathroom. "Oh, this is awful!" he wailed. "This is gonna ruin the contest!"

Carolyn snorted and said, "Not to mention ruining things for anyone who was too close to that explosion. I knew it was dangerous to have so much propane around."

"It's plenty safe as long as you're careful," Sam said. "Somebody wasn't."

"I'm sure the authorities will investigate the explosion," Phyllis said. "There's bound to be a county fire marshal or something out here. Or maybe the sheriff's department has an arson investigator. I know they do back in Parker County."

Flames were still dancing around inside the motor home, but at least they weren't leaping as high as they had been a few minutes earlier. The blaze wasn't giving off nearly as much heat, either, although what was left of the vehicle would still be too hot for anyone to approach it for a while.

Hiram Boudreau yanked off his straw hat, raked his fingers through his white hair, and turned to the crowd. "Has anybody seen Joe D.?" he asked with a note of desperate hope in his voice.

No one spoke up. Some of the assembled people shook their heads. Boudreau groaned.

The constable stepped over to Boudreau and said, "Wait a minute, Mayor. Are you saying this was Hammersmith's motor home?"

"That's right," Boudreau said. "I was just here talkin' to him yesterday. And if he's not around anywhere else, that means he must've been in there when the derned thing blew up. The cook-off doesn't have a defendin' champion anymore!"

CHAPTER 8

Boudreau seemed more upset by the trage-dy's possible effect on the cook-off than he was by the fact that Joe D. Hammersmith might well be dead. Phyllis hadn't liked Hammersmith, had, in fact, disliked the man, but he was still a human being and she wouldn't wish such a horrible fate on anyone.

"There's Josh and Felicity," Sam said, nodding toward their left.

Phyllis looked over and saw the reporter and producer from *Inside Beat*. The burly, taciturn cameraman Nick Baker was with them now, camera braced on his shoulder as he shot digital video of the crowd and the burning motor home.

Felicity was dressed in jeans and a pink t-shirt this morning, and her long brown hair was pulled back in a ponytail. To look as good as she did, she probably had to put on her makeup and get ready to face the camera as soon as she got out of bed in the morning, Phyllis thought. That constant need to be ready to go on the air would be one of the occupational hazards of the job, as far as she was concerned.

Josh wasn't nearly as put together. His shirt was untucked and his shoelaces were untied. But he didn't have to look good to do his job. He said something to Nick, then nodded to Felicity. She took a deep breath and put a concerned, solemn expression on her face as Nick swung the camera a little to frame her with the burning motor home and the crowd in the background. She started talking, although Phyllis couldn't make out the words with all the hubbub around them.

"That bunch never misses a story, do they?" Sam said.

"It's their job not to," Phyllis replied. "At least Felicity's looking properly serious."

"Acting," Carolyn said. "That TV show she works for isn't journalism. It's show business."

Phyllis couldn't disagree with that. But these days practically everything was show business.

As she looked around, she spotted several other familiar faces. Kurt Middleton, the man who had punched Hammersmith the

95

day before because he thought Hammersmith was trying to fool around with his wife, stood with his hands tucked in his hip pockets, staring intently at the destroyed motor home. An attractive woman with curly red hair stood beside him. That was probably Middleton's wife Lindy.

McKayla Carson was also there, with the tall, balding man Phyllis had guessed was her father. He had the same sort of look on his face that Middleton did, more interested than upset.

Not surprisingly, the security guard who had helped Constable Chuck during the brawl at the tavern the previous night was at the scene, too. Ken was his name, Phyllis recalled. A couple of other uniformed security officers were on hand as well.

The man who had started that tavern brawl by punching Hammersmith over gambling losses was also in the crowd. Phyllis had to think for a moment before she came up with his name: Porter. She assumed that was his last name, but she didn't really know.

So several of Hammersmith's enemies were on hand, Phyllis thought, and given the man's obvious reputation, there were probably others here with whom he had tangled in the past. That made something stir in her mind, but with a little shake of her head she pushed the idea away. She had been around too many murders, she told herself. Tragedies could happen without any ulterior motive or human agency behind them.

Hiram Boudreau was still bemoaning what had happened while the constable motioned the security officers over to him and said, "Let's get everybody cleared out of here. Ken, keep an eye on the motor home and don't let anyone near it. I don't want somebody poking around in there and getting hurt. The rest of you herd these bystanders back to their vehicles."

Ken and the others nodded in understanding and spread out to do their jobs. The crowd was already breaking up, now that the fire was mostly out, so Phyllis didn't think the officers would have any trouble dispersing the onlookers. She didn't see any reason for her and her friends to hang around, either, so she said, "Let's go on back to the trailer."

"Yeah, we might as well head for the War Wagon," Sam said. "Nothin' we can do here."

As they walked between vehicles toward the row where their borrowed travel trailer was parked, Eve said, "I wonder if the cook-off is going to continue after this."

"Why wouldn't it?" Carolyn asked. "This is a big deal. A lot of people have come hundreds, maybe even thousands of miles to participate in the contests. I can't see them being called off because of the death of one man, even if he *was* the defending champion."

"We don't know for certain that Mr. Hammersmith was killed," Phyllis pointed out. "It's going to be a while before what's left of that motor home cools down enough for the authorities to get in there and find out if there's a body."

Sam said, "Yeah, and Hammersmith might turn up somewhere else, hale and hearty, before that time comes. We'll just have to wait and see."

They went back to the breakfast they had abandoned when the explosion shook the encampment. Carolyn had put away the eggs and bacon before she and Eve left the motor home, so they could be heated up again in the microwave. She had also covered the biscuits with a clean cloth. The meal wouldn't be as good as it would have been when it was freshly made, but the food was still all right.

"You really did a good job on these biscuits, Phyllis," Carolyn commented as they ate. "You can tell they're gluten-free, but they still taste good. Excellent, in fact."

"Biscuits are biscuits," Sam said with a grin. "I never met one I didn't like, gluten or no gluten."

Eve said, "I keep reading that the idea of giving up gluten being good for you is actually a myth, unless you have that, what is it, Celiac disease."

Carolyn blew out a dismissive breath. "I know what some people say," she responded. "I also know that when I gave it up, my arthritis got a lot better. I'm convinced I would have been in a wheelchair in another ten years, or sooner, if I hadn't started being careful about what I eat."

"People have theories about a lot of things," Phyllis said. "It's what actually works that counts."

"Can't argue with reality," Sam added.

"Actually, you can," Eve said. "But then they come and take you away."

A knock sounded on the travel trailer's door as they were finishing their delayed breakfast. Sam stood up from the tiny dining table and went to answer the summons. When he opened the door, Phyllis looked past him and saw a familiar figure standing there.

"Howdy," the tall, balding man said. "Are

any of you folks entering the chili cook-off or any of the other contests?"

"I'm cookin' chili," Sam told the man, "and one of my friends here is takin' part in a couple of the side contests."

The visitor put out his hand. "My name's Wendell Carson. I'm a former contestant myself and now one of the judges."

"Sam Fletcher," Sam said as he shook hands. "What can we do for you?"

Carson said, "The judges and some of the other people who work as volunteers on the cook-off are spreading out and letting people know that all the contests will continue as scheduled, despite the, ah, tragedy earlier this morning."

Phyllis joined Sam at the door and asked, "Have they determined if anyone was hurt in the explosion?"

"Well, nobody's seen Joe D. Hammersmith, and Constable Snyder has asked around all over town. At least that's what I've heard. Investigators from the sheriff's department are supposed to be on the way. Once they get here and take a look at the scene, they may call in the Texas Rangers or the feds. They'll want to make sure this was just a terrible accident."

"Why would it be anything else?" Phyllis asked.

Wendell Carson made a face and said, "Well, not to speak ill of the maybe dead . . . but Hammersmith wasn't a well-liked man. He'd made a lot of enemies over the past few years, here at the cook-off. It would have been bad enough, him winning all the time, but he's, uh, not the easiest fella in the world to get along with."

"We sorta got that impression," Sam said. "Seemed like every time we ran into him, somebody was trying to punch him."

Carson frowned and drew in a deep breath. "I never laid a hand on him myself, but I felt like it and told him so. He knew good and well my daughter's only sixteen, but he tried to get fresh with her anyway —" He stopped short and gave a little shake of his head. "I'm sure whatever blew up and started that fire was just an accident. Don't pay any attention to anything else I said."

"We met your daughter yesterday," Phyllis said. "She seems like a very nice young lady."

"Yeah, she is. It's just . . . I'm a dad, you know? Sometimes it seems like she's too grown up for her own good." Carson took another deep breath. "Anyway, the contests are going on as planned, so I suppose I'll see you folks later. Good luck, Sam."

"Thanks. I don't envy your job, havin' to

pick out the best chili from all these cooks. I'll bet they're all pretty good."

The man grinned and said, "Yeah, it's a tough job, but somebody's got to do it."

Carson started to turn away, but Phyllis stopped him by asking, "Do you know what Mr. Hammersmith did when he wasn't entering this contest?"

"You mean his business?" Carson frowned. "I'm pretty sure he owned several new car dealerships. He was well-to-do, I know that. He didn't really need the prize money he won every year. Anyway, it's more about bragging rights than anything else. And Hammersmith could brag, that's for sure."

Carson nodded to them and went on his way. As Phyllis and Sam turned away from the door and Sam closed it, Phyllis saw Carolyn and Eve watching them intently. Carolyn said, "I know that look on your face, Phyllis, and I heard the way you were asking questions."

"You think Hammersmith was murdered," Eve added. "That someone *caused* the explosion that killed him."

Phyllis said, "I don't have any reason to think that. I was just curious, that's all."

"Curiosity leads to a murder investigation," Carolyn said.

"Only if there actually was a murder. Really, it's a lot more likely the whole thing was an accident. Anyway, if there's anything suspicious about what happened, I'm sure the local authorities will call in the Texas Rangers or the BATF, like Mr. Carson said."

Sam grinned and said, "Ol' Josh and Felicity will be disappointed if there's a murder case and you're not mixed up in it right up to your neck."

"Then they'll just have to be disappointed," Phyllis said. "Don't you have some chili to cook?"

CHAPTER 9

All of Sam's cooking gear was stored in the back of his pickup, under the camper top. He went to fetch it, driving back over from the parking area and then setting up next to the travel trailer.

By mid-morning, the air all over the encampment was full of mouth-watering aromas. Not only the spicy tang of chili cooking as contestants practiced for the competition, fine-tuning their recipes one last time, but also beans, fresh bread, even the sweet smells of cookies, pies, and cakes. Carolyn's gluten-free cornbread was in the small oven in the trailer, but the windows were open, allowing the smell of it cooking to drift out and mingle with all the other tantalizing scents.

Unfortunately, a faint whiff of ashes hung in the air, too, and Phyllis knew it came from Joe D. Hammersmith's destroyed motor home.

At the order of the sheriff's department, some of the other motor homes and trailers close to the scene of the explosion had been moved farther out in the encampment to clear the area around the blast. A couple of patrol cruisers had arrived within an hour of the explosion, followed a short time later by crime scene SUVs and a pickup belonging to the county fire marshal. A volunteer fire department truck was on hand, too, in case the blaze flared back up.

It seemed to be completely out, however, by the time Phyllis and Eve strolled over there later in the morning. Sam and Carolyn were still busy with their culinary efforts, but while Phyllis enjoyed cooking and baking as long as she was doing it, she agreed with Carolyn's assessment that it wasn't much of a spectator sport. She was also wondering if the authorities had determined anything about the blast yet.

Of course, she couldn't just waltz up and start asking questions. She and Sam worked part-time as investigators for an attorney back in Weatherford, which didn't exactly make them private detectives — although Sam liked to think that it did — but at least that gave them some semi-official status when they were looking into a case on behalf of Jimmy D'Angelo and one of his clients.

Out here in far West Texas, though, they were just civilians like anybody else. She was sure the representatives of the sheriff's department wouldn't even talk to her.

But they would have to talk to the press, at least to a certain extent, and Phyllis wasn't the least bit surprised to find Felicity, Josh, and Nick keeping tabs on the site of the explosion, although they had to stay behind the yellow crime scene tape the deputies had strung around.

"So they're calling it a crime scene now," Phyllis commented as she came up to the trio from *Inside Beat*.

Josh turned to her and said, "That's how they're treating it until they determine what caused the blast. Strictly standard procedure, they claim, but I'm not so sure."

Felicity said sharply, "Do you think this was murder, Mrs. Newsom? Do you believe someone set off the explosion on purpose? Have you picked up any clues yet?"

Phyllis noticed that Nick, who had been shooting footage of the investigation going on around the burned-out motor home, had turned and pointed the camera toward her as Felicity shot out those rapid-fire questions.

"The last I heard, they hadn't even determined if anyone was hurt yet, let alone killed," she said.

Josh grimaced and said, "Well, you can stop wondering about that. Arson investigators from the sheriff's department were able to get in there in special suits a little while ago, and they found a body under what was left of the awning Hammersmith had set up over his grill. They've already turned it over to the coroner's office."

"They wouldn't let Nick get a shot of it, either," Felicity said with a note of disappointment in her voice.

"Goodness, that would have been . . . gruesome . . . wouldn't it?" Eve said.

" 'S'okay," Nick put in. "I've seen dead bodies before."

"Actually, I meant for your viewers."

"Are you kidding?" Felicity said. "They eat that stuff up. The grosser, the better. Things aren't like they used to be."

"You're not telling us anything we don't already know," Phyllis said. After a moment, she went on, "Did anyone happen to mention if the body had been identified as being Mr. Hammersmith's?"

Josh shook his head. "One of the deputies gave us a brief statement and just said there was one fatality. No identification or indication of when we might expect to get one."

"But we'll stay on top of this breaking news," Felicity said. "They can stonewall all they want, but they won't be able to stop *Inside Beat* from getting the story."

From the dramatic tone her voice had taken on, and the way she glanced at Nick after she spoke, Phyllis had a hunch Felicity was checking to see if he had gotten her on camera while she was making that declaration.

A few more minutes went by and Phyllis was thinking about going back to the War Wagon, when a dark SUV drove into the encampment and stopped near Hammersmith's motor home. Two men got out, both wearing dark trousers, white shirts, ties, and white Stetsons. Each man had a clip-on holster with what looked like a nine-millimeter semi-automatic pistol secured in it. Phyllis didn't know a lot about guns, but she could tell that the weapons were similar to the one her son Mike carried in his work as a Parker County sheriff's deputy.

She also recognized the men by their clothing. The simple garb, not even looking much like a uniform at first glance, told her they were Texas Rangers. Their SUV was unmarked but had government plates on it.

One of the sheriff's department men came

to meet them. The officers stood there talking, and Felicity asked, "Who are those guys?"

"Texas Rangers," Phyllis said. "I'm not surprised the local authorities requested their help. State or federal investigators, or both, nearly always look into any explosion."

That perked up Felicity's interest. "Have you ever solved a murder case where something blew up like this?"

"No, but my son is a deputy, remember, and he's talked a lot about law enforcement procedures over the years."

"I'll bet you wish he was here. He could find out what's going on for you."

"It's none of my business," Phyllis said, but she felt a little hypocritical as soon as the words were out of her mouth. Somehow she had become like one of those old fire horses people used to talk about. One whiff of smoke — or in her case, one whiff of murder — and she was ready to gallop into action. Carolyn liked to make comments about how murder seemed to pop up everywhere Phyllis went, but there was some truth to that and there was no point in denying it.

The deputy spent several minutes talking to the Rangers. Quite a few people had gathered on the other side of the crime scene tape to stare at the burned-out motor home in macabre fascination. Phyllis supposed that description would apply to her just as much as it did to anybody else. She was about to turn away and suggest to Eve that they return to the travel trailer when she sensed someone looking at her. She turned her head and locked eyes with one of the white-hatted lawmen.

She wasn't sure why the Ranger was looking at her, but she met his gaze steadily. She thought that if she glanced away too abruptly, she would look guilty — even though she didn't know if there was anything to be guilty *of*.

The Ranger turned away first and said something to the deputy, but then he started walking toward Phyllis and the others. He had a slight limp, she noticed, but it didn't seem to impede him any. He covered the distance briskly, ducked under the crime scene tape — not an easy task since he was several inches above six feet in height — and nodded to them.

"I'm told you folks are part of the press," he said with a nod to Felicity, Josh, and Nick. "Which one of you is the producer?"

"That would be me," Josh said, but Felicity brushed past him and faced the tall Ranger.

"Felicity Prosper from *Inside Beat,*" she introduced herself. "If you have anything to say, you can talk to me." She motioned for Nick to keep shooting. "On the record."

"Ma'am," the Ranger said with a nod. "I just wanted to tell you that the Rangers are now in charge of this crime scene, and we won't be issuing any statements in the near future. So you might as well go on about your business of covering the chili cook-off. I assume that's why you're here in the first place."

Felicity pretty much ignored everything he had just said and continued, "You just referred to this as a crime scene, Ranger . . . What is your name, if you don't mind my asking."

It was clear from her tone and expression that she didn't really care if he minded, she expected an answer anyway.

"Culbertson, ma'am. Sergeant Martin Culbertson."

"You referred to this as a crime scene, Sergeant Culbertson. Does that mean Joe D. Hammersmith was murdered?"

"We're not issuing any statements at the moment regarding the identity of the deceased or the cause of death, other than obviously he was killed in the explosion and resulting fire. Any other determination will be made in due time."

"That sounds very much like you think it was foul play, Sergeant."

Culbertson shook his head. "Nope. All I'm saying . . . is that we're not saying. But when and if we announce anything, I'm sure you'll hear about it. In the meantime —"

"You're not going to scare us off, Ranger," Felicity interrupted him. "We're within our rights being here, as members of the press."

"As long as you stay behind that tape, you're within your rights even as citizens. Just be responsible in what you broadcast, that's all I'm asking."

"As journalists, we're always responsible," Felicity snapped.

"In a lot of ways, I would agree with you," Culbertson drawled. "The press is responsible for a lot of things. Always glad to see 'em owning up to it."

It was all Phyllis could do not to laugh. Felicity looked like she was seething at the Ranger's sly dig, but she didn't say anything else as Culbertson turned and walked back to join the other law officers. Phyllis caught Eve's eye and motioned with her head, and they started back toward the travel trailer, leaving the TV crew filling up the digital memory in Nick's camera.

"My," Eve said, "you'd have to go to

112

Central Casting to find someone who looked more like a Texas Ranger than Sergeant Culbertson!"

"You think so?" Phyllis said.

"Goodness, the man is tall and rangy and looks like he stepped out of one of those cigarette ads they used to have!"

"I didn't notice."

Eve laughed. "No offense, but I'm not sure I believe you, dear. You and Sam may have settled down comfortably into whatever sort of relationship it is you have, but you've still got eyes in your head. If Mr. Hammersmith really was murdered, someone's going to have to get to the bottom of it, and I don't see any reason why it shouldn't be you!"

Phyllis was about to argue with her, but just then someone behind her called, "Ma'am?"

She stopped and turned and saw Sergeant Martin Culbertson walking toward them.

CHAPTER 10

"He can't be talking to us," Phyllis said.

"No, he's talking to *you*," Eve said with a smile. "I just wish that big, handsome Ranger was striding purposefully toward me."

Phyllis cast a quick glare in her direction, then moved forward to meet Sergeant Culbertson, who, judging by his face and actions, was indeed bent on talking to her.

As they came up to each other and stopped, Culbertson lifted his right hand and tapped a finger against his hat brim in a polite greeting. "Ma'am," he said again. "Excuse me for bothering you."

"You're not bothering me," Phyllis said honestly.

"You were with those TV folks, weren't you? Do you work with them?"

She shook her head and said, "No, we're just acquainted, that's all."

"I thought when I saw you standing there

in the crowd that you looked familiar. It took me a few minutes to remember where I'd seen you before. Actually, I've only seen pictures of you." He paused. "You're Phyllis Newsom, aren't you?"

She was flustered for a moment by the idea that this Texas Ranger had recognized her, but then she thought she didn't have any reason to let it bother her. She hadn't done anything wrong.

"That's right, I am," she said. "This is my friend Eve Turner."

Sergeant Culbertson nodded and ticked a finger against his hat brim to Eve, too. "Miz Turner."

"Hello, Sergeant," Eve said with the brilliant smile that appeared by habit any time she was talking to a handsome, possibly eligible male over the age of fifty.

The wattage seemed to be wasted on Culbertson, though, who turned his attention back to Phyllis and went on, "I've read quite a bit about your career."

"As a junior high school history teacher, you mean?"

A smile tugged at Culbertson's mouth under the neatly trimmed mustache. "I think you know that's not what I'm talking about, ma'am. When it comes to clearing homicides, you've got a record I and a lot of my fellow Rangers would envy."

Phyllis shook her head and said, "The authorities have cleared those crimes. I've just helped out a little now and then."

"If you call figuring out who the killer is and finding the evidence to convict helping out, then yeah, I'd say you have. Every murderer you've gone after has been brought to justice. And don't say you've been lucky. That would be false modesty."

"I seem to have a knack for what I do," Phyllis said. "What exactly did you want to talk to me about, Sergeant?"

Culbertson pointed with a thumb toward the burned-out motor home behind him. "This is an open case with the circumstances yet to be determined. Like I told the press, the Rangers are in charge of it. And we don't need any help."

"So you're warning me to keep my nose out, is that it?"

"Well, I wouldn't put it quite that bluntly," Culbertson said with a shrug. "But I suppose that's what it amounts to. Poking around in an official investigation as a civilian will only get you in trouble."

"I probably shouldn't say this," Eve spoke up, "but Phyllis has heard *that* before!"

"Yeah, I know. What is they call you on TV, Mrs. Newsom? The crime-busting grandma?"

"So you *have* seen Felicity's stories on *Inside Beat*," Phyllis said.

Culbertson shrugged again. "I'm just trying to do the right thing here," he said. "I don't want you causing a bunch of trouble for yourself."

"Or for you."

"You won't be causing any trouble for me. I do my job either way, no matter what comes."

"Yes, I expect you do," Phyllis said. "Well, you don't have to worry, Sergeant. I have no personal stake in this case, no reason to get involved. I met Mr. Hammersmith a couple of times, that's all. And I didn't like him." She smiled. "Does that make me a suspect?"

"Not likely," the Ranger said. "If it did, practically everybody who's in Cactus Bluff this weekend would —" He stopped short and took a deep breath. "Just remember what I said, that's all."

Culbertson turned and walked away, his limp noticeable but just barely.

"Am I mistaken," Eve said to Phyllis, "or did you just trick him into admitting that the victim was Joe D. Hammersmith?"

"It's not much of an admission," Phyllis said. "Everything we'd seen and heard so far this morning pointed to the fact that Hammersmith was killed in the explosion. And the sergeant is right about there not being any shortage of suspects. I can think of several without really trying, and I'm sure you can, too."

"Such as everyone who took a punch at him?"

"That's where I'd start . . . *if* his death turns out to be murder. There's still a better than average chance it was an accident."

"Yes, of course," Eve said, but she didn't sound convinced of that.

When they got back to the travel trailer, they found Sam outside stirring a pot of chili as it simmered on the propane-fueled grill he had set up earlier. He bent over it, inhaled the aroma coming from it, and then grinned at Phyllis.

"You gotta come smell this," he said.

"That sounds like the set-up for a joke," Eve said. "At least he didn't ask you to pull his finger."

"No joke," Sam said. "Just good chili."

Phyllis drew in a good whiff of the chili and nodded. "It does smell good," she said. "How soon can we have a taste?"

"Oh, it'll have to simmer for a good long while yet. The meat needs to be good and tender. We can try it out this afternoon, I

118

reckon."

"Meanwhile," Carolyn said from the trailer's open door, "my cornbread is ready, and I have a pot of beans cooking. We can have that for lunch."

Eve asked, "Are you going to save some of the beans to put in the chili?"

Sam stared at her, completely aghast.

"What?" Eve said. "Did I say something wrong?"

"Real chili cooks don't put beans in their red. That's another way to get disqualified. You can have a side of beans, if you want to. Especially if you put chow-chow on the beans and eat 'em with cornbread." Sam looked at Carolyn. "You got chow-chow, don't you?"

"Of course," she said.

Eve shook her head. "I've lived in Texas most of my life, and some things are just still beyond me, I suppose, especially when it comes to food."

"Don't worry about it," Phyllis told her. "Evidently chili aficionados have their own rules and customs."

Sam said, "And you should be thankful for that, because it makes for mighty good chili."

"Not to change the subject," Eve went on, "but the Texas Rangers have arrived and taken over the Hammersmith case."

"It's an actual case now?" Carolyn asked.

"And they know it was Hammersmith who was killed?" Sam added.

Phyllis nodded in answer to both of those questions. "They haven't ruled the death either a homicide or an accident yet, but they seem sure Hammersmith was the victim."

Eve said, "Yes, Phyllis got one of the Rangers to admit that. A very good-looking Ranger, I might add."

Sam cocked an eyebrow. "Is that so?"

"He wasn't *that* good-looking," Phyllis said. She considered. "Ruggedly handsome, maybe."

"No maybe about it," Eve said.

"Well, why don't you go after him, then, and quit harassing Phyllis about it?" Carolyn asked.

"She knows I'm not serious. Don't you, dear?"

Phyllis had had enough of the conversation, so she said, "Of course," and stepped up into the trailer. Even though the explosion that had claimed Joe D. Hammersmith's life had been quite a distraction, she had learned quite a bit about the chili cookoff and how it was set up and run. She thought it might be a good idea to go ahead and get some notes down for her magazine article while everything was still fresh in her mind.

She got out her laptop and worked on that for the next hour. The smells that filled the air were pretty distracting, but she forced herself to buckle down and work. She was more than ready for a break, though, when Carolyn announced that lunch was ready.

The beans were well-cooked, Carolyn having put them on to soak the night before, and there was a bowl of lightly sweetened pickled cabbage, onion, green tomatoes, chopped green and red bell peppers on the counter — Sam's "chow-chow" — to add to them according to each person's taste. Phyllis had found the chow-chow in a country convenience store and bought several jars. Carolyn had cut and buttered thick squares of cornbread.

It was as simple and old-fashioned — and good — a meal as anyone could find, Phyllis thought as she, Carolyn, and Eve ate around the little table. Sam hadn't come inside. He wasn't going to leave his chili unattended, so Phyllis had fixed a plate for him and taken it outside, along with a big plastic glass of iced tea. He ate his lunch sitting in one of the folding lawn chairs he had set up beside the grill.

"Mighty good cornbread, Carolyn," Sam called through the open door. "Is this more of that gluten-free stuff?"

"Yes, it is," she said. "It's fairly easy to make gluten-free cornbread, and it turns out well. Just like gluten-free pasta." Carolyn shook her head. "It's just a shame that no one seems to be able to make a decent gluten-free sandwich bread. All of it that I've tried has ranged from mediocre to terrible."

"Don't you miss pies and cakes?" Eve asked.

"Certainly. But I don't miss my joints hurting so bad I want to cry. And that's what rheumatoid arthritis does when gluten causes it to flare up."

Phyllis didn't know how valid the medical science of Carolyn's claim was, but as far as she was concerned, if her friend felt better, that was all that mattered. And as Carolyn had said, many of the gluten-free foods were quite good. It was just a matter of avoiding the ones that weren't.

They were cleaning up after the meal when Sam said, "Hey, Phyllis, here come Felicity and Josh."

She stepped into the doorway and saw the TV reporter and producer walking along the open space between the rows of motor homes and travel trailers. Felicity's hair was down now and she wore a stylish top instead of the t-shirt she'd had on earlier.

"The county sheriff's office just issued a statement," Felicity said as she and Josh came up to the War Wagon. "The Rangers may be in charge of the case, but they're letting the sheriff talk to the press. I guess so they won't be bothered as much. Anyway, they've officially identified Hammersmith as the victim and confirmed that the blast originated with the propane grill he was going to use to cook his chili."

"The Hammersmith Deluxe," Josh put in. "That's what he called his chili."

"We know that, Josh," Felicity said. She turned her attention back to Phyllis and Sam. "The propane cylinder on the grill exploded, then the propane tank attached to the motor home exploded, and then the gas tank blew."

Sam nodded and said, "That's the way we had it figured. Three separate explosions, but so close together it almost sounded like one."

"But here's the interesting part . . . the spokesman for the sheriff's department said that the cause of the first explosion is undetermined at this time." Felicity smirked. "You know what that means, don't you?"

"That they haven't determined what caused it?" Phyllis said.

"That it was *murder*! If it was an accident, they would have said so."

Sam said, "I think you're jumpin' the gun there a little. The authorities don't like to announce anything, one way or the other, until they're sure. So it makes more sense that they're *not* sure."

"Oh, come on," Felicity scoffed. "Hammersmith was a son of a . . . he was not a nice man. I only had one drink with him, and I could tell that."

"And yet you came to his defense during that brawl at the tavern," Phyllis said.

"Of course. Just because I thought the guy was a sleaze didn't mean I was going to stand by and let him get knocked out of the competition. He was the defending champ! I still needed to get an on-camera interview with him. But that doesn't change the fact that nobody liked him and a lot of people had grudges against him. Every one of those grudges is a motive for murder."

Sam raked a thumbnail along his jawline, frowned, and asked, "You really think somebody could have rigged up that explosion?"

"Let's ask the expert on murder," Felicity said. "Phyllis, do you think that's possible?"

Phyllis didn't waste her breath trying to disabuse Felicity of the notion that she was an expert on murder. Already the wheels of her brain had been turning over while the young woman was talking, and now she said, "I don't really know much about those grills, but it seems plausible that someone who uses them all the time might know a way to make one blow up."

"Yeah, I was just thinkin' the same thing," Sam admitted. "I hate to think a fellow chili cook would stoop so low as to do such a thing, though."

"So we've established motive and means. That leaves opportunity." Felicity gave a brittle laugh and waved a perfectly manicured hand. "Just look around. In this madhouse, somebody could do all sorts of things without anyone else noticing."

She was right about that, too, Phyllis thought. Any other time of the year, Cactus Bluff was sleepy and mostly deserted, so any kind of troublemaker would stand out. But on this weekend, a killer would have no trouble blending into the crowd.

"I can see it on your face," Felicity went on. "You know as well as I do that Joe D. Hammersmith was murdered. That just leaves one question."

"Who killed him?" Phyllis asked.

"No." Felicity smiled. "How are you going to track down the killer so that we can follow you every step of the way?"

CHAPTER 11

"I never said I was going to try to find the killer," Phyllis pointed out.

"No, but everybody here is well aware of what you've done in the past. You can't resist the challenge of a good murder to solve, Mrs. Newsom."

"A *good* murder?" Carolyn repeated. "Isn't that an oxymoron?"

"You know what I mean," Felicity said. "You've got a despicable victim and all these suspects who might have wanted him dead. This case reminds me of what happened at that elementary school carnival a few years ago. I read about that one. In fact, I read about all the murders you've solved, Mrs. Newsom. Don't you want to see the killer brought to justice?"

Phyllis didn't say anything for a moment. Then she told Felicity, "The Rangers have warned me to stay out of it. I've already been arrested once for getting mixed up in an open investigation when I was told not to. I'd just as soon not repeat the experience."

"They can't lock you up if you're working for *Inside Beat*," Felicity argued. "Freedom of the press."

"Journalists get put in jail all the time," Carolyn said. "Not often enough to suit some of us."

Felicity ignored that comment and went on, "I'll call the executive producer and get him to hire you as a consultant, Mrs. Newsom. Mr. Fletcher, too, if you'd like. That way you'll have the constitutional right to ask questions, whether the authorities like it or not." She paused. "There are half a dozen other media outlets here covering the chili cook-off, and now they're covering the murder, too. But if you work with us, we'll be the only ones who have you on our side, and you'll be part of the story, too."

"What if I don't *want* to be part of the story?" Phyllis asked.

Felicity scoffed and shook her head. "Too late for that. You're well-known in the true crime community, and you're here on the scene of a spectacular murder. We'll be playing up that angle, and so will all the other media once they get wind of it. But if you're working exclusively with us, we can shield you from being harassed by them, at least to a certain extent."

Eve said, "That sounds suspiciously like blackmail, dear."

"I think it's more like extortion," Felicity said calmly, "but call it whatever you want to. It just makes sense for you to throw in with us, Phyllis."

She hated to admit it, but Felicity might have a point. On the other hand . . .

"It's going to knock the props right out from under your argument if it turns out the explosion really was an accident," Phyllis said.

"I'm willing to take that chance," Felicity replied with a smile. "What do you say?"

"I'll have to think about it. And you'll have to call your boss and make sure he'll even go along with the idea."

"He will." Felicity's smile became a confident smirk. "I can be very persuasive."

"That's true," Josh said with a nod. "She can be."

The idea of working for one of those lurid, celebrity-obsessed tabloid TV shows rubbed Phyllis the wrong way. But she supposed it wouldn't hurt to at least consider it. In the meantime, the whole thing might become moot. So in a way she was just stalling to give that a chance to happen when she told

Felicity, "Check with your boss and then get back to me."

"Fair enough. But I know when you think about it, you'll see that I'm right." Felicity motioned curtly at her companion as she turned away from the trailer. "Come on, Josh."

As the two of them walked off, Carolyn said quietly, "There he goes again, following her like a little puppy dog. Doesn't he realize that sooner or later she's just going to kick him again?"

Eve said, "A man has to come to that realization in his own time. Josh is smart enough to figure it out sooner or later."

"Or else he'll pine after her futilely for the rest of his life."

"Then that's his business, isn't it, dear?"

Carolyn just grunted, then said, "I need to put up the rest of that cornbread."

Phyllis sat down in the lawn chair next to Sam's and asked him, "What do you think I should do?"

"You mean about workin' with Felicity and Josh?"

"That's right."

He shrugged. "I reckon she's probably overestimatin' the amount of leeway that would get you with the sheriff and the Rangers. But at the same time, it can't hurt to have the press on your side." A grin stretched across his rugged face. "Who knows, it might lead to a whole new career for you. You might wind up hostin' one of those shows, like that fella from that old high school sitcom. Then you could spend all your time talkin' about Kardashians and stuff like that."

A shudder went through Phyllis. "Don't even think that. Anyway, it would never happen. Felicity has her eye set on that job, and she'd stab anybody who got in her way in the back."

"More than likely," Sam agreed. He stood up to stir his chili and check on its progress.

They sat there chatting idly for a while. Carolyn and Eve came out of the trailer to join them. People walking by stopped to talk to Sam about his chili. The subject of the explosion often came up, too, and the rumor that Joe D. Hammersmith was the victim had gone through the entire encampment and seemingly been accepted as fact.

However, with the cook-off going on, most people tended to turn their attention away from what had happened and toward the contest itself. Murder was tragic and sensational, of course, but chili was chili and they had their priorities straight.

Phyllis didn't mind the lull. It gave her

time to think, and more importantly it gave the law time to settle the case so that she didn't need to become involved.

Sam broke into the reverie that settled over her by drawling, "Looks like a star packer comin'."

She had heard him talk about Western novels enough to understand what he meant. She looked the same way he was looking and saw Ranger Sergeant Martin Culbertson walking toward them. He wasn't just strolling along, either. He struck her as the sort who always had some distinct purpose in whatever he did.

He came up to them, nodded, and pinched his hat brim. "Mrs. Newsom," he said.

"Sergeant Culbertson," Phyllis said. "What can I do for you?"

"Nothing right now, ma'am. I came to talk to your friend here." The Ranger turned to Sam. "You're Sam Fletcher, sir?"

"I am." Sam stood up and extended his hand. "Pleasure to meet you, Sergeant."

"I'd like to ask you a few questions, Mr. Fletcher, if you don't mind."

Sam shrugged and said, "Sure."

"Wait a minute," Carolyn said. "Is this an interrogation? Are you questioning Sam in an official capacity, Sergeant?"

Culbertson smiled, but Phyllis thought she

could see in his eyes that he was a little irritated by Carolyn's question. "I'm just talking to him, ma'am. And you are . . . ?"

"Carolyn Wilbarger," she said. "And if you want to ask me anything more than that, I'll have to have a lawyer present. And I think Sam should, too, before you interrogate him."

"Nobody said this was an interrogation —"

"A law enforcement officer asking questions can't very well be anything else, can it?" Carolyn shot back.

Carolyn had always been skeptical of the authorities, to say the least. She had a skeptical nature, period. And some previous experiences with the law had only strengthened that tendency in her.

Sam half-turned and held out a hand toward Carolyn in a placating gesture as he said, "It's all right, I don't mind talkin' to the sergeant. It's not like I've got anything to hide, after all." He smiled. "Unless it's my chili recipe you're after, Sergeant, and if it is, I might have to stand on my right not to share that."

"I'm not sure you have that right," Culbertson said.

"Oh, I think there's somethin' in the Constitution about chili. At least in Texas there is."

Phyllis thought she saw a flicker of amusement on Culbertson's face, but then it went away and was replaced by a much more serious expression. He said, "I came to talk to you about Joe D. Hammersmith, Mr. Fletcher."

"I'm not sure what I can tell you. I met the man for the first time yesterday. I'd seen his name on the cook-off's website because he's won for the past few years, but that's all I ever knew about him."

"Then what were you doing at his motor home last night?"

Phyllis had to work hard not to show her surprise at Culbertson's sharply voiced question. She managed to control her reaction, but Carolyn didn't.

"That's it," Carolyn said as she stood up. "Don't say another word to this man, Sam. If he wants to know anything else, he can question you officially, with a lawyer present. Don't let him get away with this folksy 'just talking' business."

"My lawyer's hundreds of miles away in Weatherford," Sam said, referring to Jimmy D'Angelo. "I don't figure he could get here until tomorrow, if he was able to come at all."

"The Rangers can just wait, then," Carolyn declared.

Phyllis understood why her friend was so adamant. A part of her agreed with Carolyn. Culbertson had definitely had a suspicious edge in his voice when he asked that question. But he had also sounded sure of his footing. Did he have a witness claiming that Sam had been at Hammersmith's motor home the previous night? Sam had been with her, Carolyn, and Eve all evening, so the only time he could have visited Hammersmith was after he left the three of them here at the travel trailer. Phyllis couldn't conceive of any reason for him to have done that . . . and even if he had, wouldn't he have said something about it this morning, especially after the explosion that killed Hammersmith?

"How about it, Mr. Fletcher?" Culbertson asked. "You can clear the whole thing up right now, and we won't have to worry about it anymore."

"Not a word, Sam," Carolyn repeated.

Sam took a deep breath, then said, "Carolyn, I know you're just tryin' to look out for me, but I really don't see any reason to drag lawyers into this." He turned to Culbertson. "Sergeant, I'm not stayin' here in the War Wagon with the ladies. I've got a pickup with a camper on it, over in the parkin' area.

After I left Phyllis, Carolyn, and Eve here yesterday evenin', I walked back over there to turn in. That's why I went past Hammersmith's motor home."

"I've been told you didn't just walk past it," Culbertson said. "A witness told me you stopped there for five or ten minutes and were messing around with the set-up he was going to use to cook his chili today."

"Who told you that?" Carolyn demanded.

"I can't say, ma'am."

Carolyn waved a hand dismissively. "Then such a claim is worthless. The person's lying, whoever it is."

Phyllis was watching Sam's face, though, and she knew in that moment that Culbertson's witness *wasn't* lying. She could tell by the way Sam grimaced slightly.

He didn't look away from the Ranger, though. He met Culbertson's challenging stare squarely and said, "I was there, all right, but you've got a couple of things wrong, Sergeant. First off, I had no idea that motor home belonged to Hammersmith. I didn't know whose it was. And I wasn't there for any ten minutes, or even five. Three, maybe four at the outside, I'd say. But I really don't think it was even that long."

"Then why did you stop?"

"The simplest reason in the world," Sam said with a shrug. "I was lookin' at his set-up. It was a dang nice grill. A lot fancier than this one." He poked a thumb at his own grill with the pot of chili simmering on it. "But I'm willin' to bet what I'm cookin' up on this one will taste just as good or better."

Culbertson shook his head and said, "That's not my area of expertise. Did you touch Hammersmith's grill or anything else around there?"

"Not that I recall. If I did, it was just so I could take a better look. I didn't hurt anything."

Phyllis said, "You've found evidence of sabotage, haven't you, Sergeant? Otherwise you wouldn't be asking these particular questions."

"I'm not at liberty to answer that, Mrs. Newsom."

Eve said, "But Phyllis is right, or else you'd be able to say so, wouldn't you, Sergeant?"

Culbertson just set his jaw a little tighter and didn't say anything for a moment. Then he turned back to Sam and went on, "You were in the crowd around the scene of the explosion this morning. Why didn't you come forward and tell anyone that you'd been there last night?"

Carolyn snorted and said, "Your crude attempt to railroad him is answer enough for that, I think."

"Nobody's bein' railroaded," Sam said. "When we walked over there after the blast this mornin', the idea that it could've been the same motor home where I stopped last night didn't even occur to me. For one thing, it was dark last night. I didn't pay that much attention to the other RVs around. But there was a light set up to shine on the grill, I guess to keep people from messin' with it. Like I told you, I took a look for a minute or two and then walked on. Didn't think any more about it."

"Not even when you saw the motor home on fire this morning?"

"Things look different in the daylight," Sam said. "Now, I'll admit that after we came back over here and I started cookin' up this batch of chili, I had time to think and I wondered if it was the same motor home. But I knew I hadn't done anything wrong, so I didn't really worry about it."

Culbertson nodded slowly. "Those are good answers, Mr. Fletcher. The sort of answers that an honest man would give."

"That's what I've always tried to be."

"You're going to be here all weekend for

the cook-off, right?"

"I plan on makin' it to the finals," Sam said. "Heck, I plan on winnin', but I guess time will tell about that."

"Time will tell about most things," Culbertson said. He nodded to Phyllis, Carolyn, and Eve, added, "Ladies," and then walked off.

"Sam, that man believes you killed Hammersmith!" Carolyn said when the Ranger was out of earshot.

"Now, he didn't *say* that —"

"But we could all tell that's what he was thinking. Isn't that right, Phyllis?"

She hesitated for a second, then answered, "He did seem pretty suspicious of you, Sam."

"We believe you're completely innocent, though, dear," Eve said.

"Of course we do," Carolyn said. "Hammersmith may have been a jackass in general, but you didn't have any particular trouble with him, Sam. Other than maybe wanting to beat him in the cook-off. And nobody would resort to murder to win a chili cook-off!"

Phyllis wanted to believe that was true, but the more time she spent around some of the people in Cactus Bluff this weekend, the less sure she was of that. The idea was far-fetched, without a doubt, but could it be ruled out? She didn't know.

"Yeah, but they got a witness puttin' me on the scene of the crime," Sam said. "Things like that carry a lot of weight with the law. And they can prove I at least met Hammersmith, because plenty of folks must've seen us talkin' to him yesterday evenin'. The way the Rangers'll look at it, me and Hammersmith might've argued about something and caused enough hard feelin's for me to go after him."

"That's insane," Carolyn insisted.

Insane it might be, Phyllis thought, but more than once she had seen people she knew to be innocent accused of murder and arrested. It seemed unlikely that the Rangers could make more than the thinnest of cases against Sam . . . but even that slight possibility was worrisome.

A new voice broke into her thoughts. Felicity was approaching and had called her name. Josh hurried along beside the leggy reporter.

"I've talked to the executive producer," Felicity said. "He's willing to hire both of you as special correspondents, Phyllis. All you and Sam have to do is say yes, and you'll have all the power of *Inside Beat* behind you."

Phyllis wasn't sure how much actual power that would amount to, but it had to be more than what they would wield as civilians. She looked at Sam, who shrugged and said, "It's up to you."

She didn't want that cloud of unjust suspicion hanging over him. That wasn't right or fair, and she knew the quickest and best way to dispel that cloud would be to uncover the truth.

"All right," she said. "If it turns out to be murder" — and the way Sergeant Culbertson had been acting when he questioned Sam, how could it be anything but? — "we'll do what we can to find the killer."

"And *Inside Beat* gets the exclusive story?" Felicity asked eagerly.

Phyllis nodded. "*Inside Beat* gets the story."

CHAPTER 12

Later that afternoon, Phyllis and Sam walked over to the scene of the explosion again. The burned debris, all that was left of the motor home, had cooled enough that the investigators didn't have to wear special suits to poke around in it. Phyllis noted, however, that they still had on thick-soled boots to protect their feet, as well as thick gloves on their hands. Of course, crime scene investigators always wore gloves of some sort to protect any evidence they might find.

People still stood behind the yellow crime scene tape looking on curiously. Phyllis spotted a familiar face and drifted over toward a rawboned man with reddish-brown hair. She nodded to him and said with an air of pleasant but idle curiosity, "That motor home belonged to Joe D. Hammersmith, didn't it?"

"Yeah," the man said. "I hear he got

burned up in it." He shrugged. "Wish I could say I was sorry, but I'd be lyin'."

"He wasn't a friend of yours?"

"Not hardly. Fella won eight hundred bucks from me in a poker game at last year's cook-off, and I'm convinced he cheated."

"That's terrible."

"Yeah, I thought so." The man glanced at her curiously. "You in the chili competition?"

"No, but a friend of mine is. My name's Phyllis Newsom."

"Jeff Porter," the man supplied his name, a natural reaction when someone else has just introduced themselves, as Phyllis knew quite well.

"Have you been competing in the cook-off for long?"

"Five years. Ever since the first one."

"How have you done?"

"Finished fourth one year." Porter shrugged. "That's the highest I've ever placed . . . although I think I deserved to win a time or two."

Phyllis smiled. "I'm sure all the contestants feel that way."

The grim lines on Porter's face relaxed a little as he said, "Yeah, I guess. Who's your friend who's in the contest?"

"Sam Fletcher. That's him over there."

Porter looked at Sam and nodded. "Fella looks familiar. He been in the cook-off before?"

"No, this is his first year."

"Well, I'd wish him luck, but I plan to win this year, so I won't. Maybe I'll actually have a chance, now that Hammersmith's not gonna be in it."

"Wouldn't everyone have a chance anyway?"

Porter hesitated, then said, "There have been rumors that not everything's on the up and up when it comes to the judging."

Phyllis managed to look shocked. "Are you saying that the cook-off might be rigged?"

"Nobody knows that for sure. Hammersmith and Hiram Boudreau have always been good buddies, though. And there's no denying that Hammersmith winning was good publicity for the contest. He was always the loud, flashy sort, quick to mouth off about how good he was. The press likes that, you know. Controversy always gets a lot of attention."

"That's true," Phyllis said, nodding as if that had never occurred to her.

"But now the competition is wide open, for sure. May the best man win." Porter laughed. "And that's gonna be me."

"Best man," Phyllis repeated. "Don't any women enter the contest?"

"Well, sure, there are a few. But cooking chili . . . that's sort of a manly thing, you know."

Phyllis certainly could have argued that point, but she didn't really see any point in it at this particular time. She was more interested in what Porter had said about the possibility that Hammersmith won the cook-off every year through nefarious means. Royce Glennister had already accused Hammersmith of cheating. It seemed to be a widespread belief that the man hadn't won his championships fair and square.

That still didn't strike Phyllis as a reasonable motive for murder . . . but a motive didn't have to seem reasonable to an outsider.

Only to a murderer.

Porter nodded to Phyllis and then walked off, evidently having seen enough of the explosion site. Sam joined her a minute later and said, "That's the fella who punched Hammersmith at the tavern last night, wasn't it?"

"Yes. His name is Jeff Porter."

"I figured you might be tryin' to snooker a little information out of him. That's why I kept my distance and didn't interrupt y'all. Did you find out anything?"

"Only that some of the contestants suspect that the cook-off is rigged."

Sam's eyebrows rose. "Really? Just because Hammersmith won for three years in a row? Sounds a little like sour grapes to me. Of course, any time somebody dominates a sport for a while, folks start to think they've been cheatin'. You heard what Royce said last night about Hammersmith precookin'."

"Mr. Porter seems confident that his chili is going to win, now that Hammersmith is gone."

"So you're thinkin' Porter rigged that explosion to get rid of him?"

Phyllis shook her head. "It's too early to think anything like that. But it's one more thing to consider, too."

The rest of the afternoon passed uneventfully, if you didn't count tasting the chili Sam had cooked. It was delicious, just as Phyllis expected. Carolyn praised the results, too, but then said, "We're going to get awfully tired of eating chili before this weekend is over, aren't we?"

"Not just the weekend," Sam replied with a smile. "I'm gonna freeze all the leftovers.

We'll be havin' chili casseroles and Frito pie and chili on our hot dogs for a good long spell."

"I can't wait," Carolyn said dryly. "Although if not for all those uses for leftover chili, I wouldn't have recipes to enter in the other contests, would I?"

They made supper on the chili and the leftover cornbread and beans from lunch, then got ready to attend the opening ceremonies and concert that evening. Sam returned to his pickup and camper to put on a nicer shirt, while Phyllis, Carolyn, and Eve dressed up more, too. Phyllis matched a black shell with some white slacks and slipped on some black and white strappy sandals. Carolyn changed into a blue skirt with a matching top. She put on some silver low-heeled shoes and added a chunky silver necklace. Eve embraced color. She put on a Hawaiian print fitted dress and completed it with a short-sleeved fitted jacket. As the three women left the travel trailer, Felicity, Josh, and Nick walked up, with Nick carrying his camera as usual. Felicity was on at least her third outfit of the day, a Western shirt and skirt that Dale Evans might have worn, except that the skirt was a lot shorter than anything the Queen of the Cowgirls would have considered decent.

"I thought we'd all go to the opening ceremonies together," Felicity said. "Where's Sam?"

"He should be back any minute," Phyllis said.

"You haven't solved the murder yet, have you?"

"What? No."

"Be sure to call me as soon as you do, if we're not around already. Remember, you're working for *Inside Beat* now."

"I'll keep that in mind," Phyllis said. She was starting to have a few regrets about agreeing to Felicity's suggestion.

A few more minutes went by, and Sam didn't show up. Phyllis wasn't actually worried about him, but she did wonder where he was. Felicity was impatient to get to the big tent, so after a little longer, Phyllis said, "Why don't all of you go ahead? I'll check at Sam's pickup and make sure there's nothing wrong, then we'll meet you there."

"I can come with you," Carolyn said. "I'm not sure you should be wandering around this place by yourself, Phyllis."

"I'll be perfectly fine," Phyllis insisted. "You and Eve go on with Felicity and Josh and Nick."

"Well, if you're sure . . ."

"I am," Phyllis said.

The others headed toward the big tent, Carolyn still with some visible reluctance, while Phyllis went the other way toward the parking area where she hoped to find Sam. He might have had trouble deciding what to wear, she mused, although that wasn't like him. He never worried much about such things.

She was passing one of the travel trailers when she heard angry voices coming from inside. Something was familiar about one of them. A man and woman were arguing, and Phyllis thought the man's voice belonged to Kurt Middleton.

That was confirmed when she heard him say, "Damn it, Lindy, I knew you were playing around with Hammersmith again!"

"That's not true," Middleton's wife replied. She was trying to sound indignant, Phyllis thought as she slowed, but she didn't quite pull it off. There was a hint of defensiveness in her tone. Phyllis had no idea if Lindy Middleton had been having an affair with Hammersmith, but she wasn't exactly being honest with her husband, either, Phyllis sensed.

She straightened her back and moved on at a quicker pace. She hadn't yet been reduced to eavesdropping on wrangling couples, and since there didn't seem to be any violence going on other than verbal, she wasn't going to lurk around outside the Middletons' trailer.

She wondered, however, what had happened to make Kurt Middleton even more convinced that he was right about his wife and Joe D. Hammersmith. Middleton had sounded like he'd discovered something he considered to be proof . . .

Those thoughts disappeared from her brain as she spotted the figures of two tall men up ahead. Sam was one of them, Ranger Sergeant Martin Culbertson the other. Phyllis's heart started to beat a little faster. But Sam wasn't in handcuffs, she noted, and the two men didn't seem to be upset, so she cautioned herself not to over-react.

When they saw her coming, they stopped talking to each other and waited for her. Phyllis came up to them, managed to smile, and said, "I wondered what was keeping you, Sam. Now I see it was *who,* not *what.*"

"Oh, I'm not keeping him," Culbertson said. "Mr. Fletcher's not in custody. We were just talking."

"That's right," Sam said.

"New developments on the case?" Phyllis asked.

Culbertson smiled and said, "I'm afraid I

can't discuss that."

"But you can with Sam?"

"I never said that's what we were talking about."

"The sergeant was askin' me about my chili recipe," Sam said. "I think he's givin' some thought to enterin' the cook-off next year."

Phyllis said, "Is that so?"

"I've been known to cook up a decent pot of red," Culbertson said. "Are you folks headed to the opening ceremonies and the concert?"

"That's right."

"I believe I'll head that way myself. Mind if I walk along with you?"

Phyllis did mind. She wanted to ask Sam what was going on, because she didn't believe for a second that they had been discussing chili recipes. If Culbertson accompanied them, she couldn't find out what the real scoop was.

On the other hand, she couldn't see any way to refuse what he had phrased as a friendly request without seeming hostile or suspicious, so she said, "That's fine."

They started toward the big tent with Sam on one side of her and Culbertson on the other. Phyllis was glad that Eve wasn't here. If her friend had seen that, she would have been bound to make some sort of comment.

A lot of people were headed in the same direction. The sun hadn't set yet, but the opening ceremonies would get underway around eight o'clock, with the concert to follow at approximately nine.

Phyllis saw Constable Chuck Snyder's Jeep parked near the tent but didn't see the young lawman himself. She spotted the security officer named Ken standing at the tent's entrance, however, looking over the people as they came in. Ken's expression was wary, as if he were on the watch for trouble, which was probably the case. After the explosion that had killed the cook-off's defending champion, everyone had to be at least a little on edge.

Ropes had been strung between the tent's support poles to create a wall of sorts, although those barriers wouldn't keep anybody out. It would be easy to duck under the ropes. But people usually tended to do what was expected of them, so the crowd flowed toward the marked entrance at one end of the tent where Ken was posted. Phyllis, Sam, and Culbertson joined the stream of humanity.

When they got inside, Phyllis looked for Carolyn, Eve, and the trio from *Inside Beat*. The night before, Hiram Boudreau had said they could sit up front, so Phyllis nodded to Sam and pointed in that direction.

Sergeant Culbertson said, "I'll see you folks later," and drifted away in the crowd.

"Take it easy, Sergeant," Sam called after him.

"What in the world was that man after now?" Phyllis asked as she linked her arm with Sam's and leaned closer to him. Everyone in the tent was talking, it seemed like, so the air was full of sounds and the background noise made it more difficult for her to hear.

"You mean the Ranger?" Sam said. "We were just talkin' about chili —"

"I'm sorry, Sam. The sergeant doesn't seem like the type to engage in casual conversation."

"Well . . ." With obvious reluctance, Sam went on, "He didn't come right out and say it, but the impression I got is that they found a piece of Hammersmith's grill that survived the blast. And they pulled a fingerprint off of it."

"A fingerprint?" Phyllis repeated. "You don't mean . . ."

"From the way the sergeant was actin', I'd say there's a good chance that print belongs to me."

CHAPTER 13

Phyllis stopped and stared up at him. "That's insane," she said. "You wouldn't —"

"Blow a fella up?" Sam laughed a little and shook his head. "No, I'm not really the explosive type."

"You're not a murderer, and anyone who knows you would never have any doubts about that." Something occurred to Phyllis. "Anyway, you admitted that you looked at Hammersmith's grill. You probably got your fingerprint on it then."

"I lifted the lid," Sam said. "Probably shouldn't have. I wouldn't like it if some stranger was pokin' around my stuff. But it was just innocent curiosity, that's all. I was admirin' the blasted thing."

"Innocent is the key word here," Phyllis said. "Did you explain that to Sergeant Culbertson?"

"Oh, we never got around to speakin' that

plain about the deal. It was more, what's the word, oblique than that. The Ranger knows that if he comes right out and accuses me of something, I'm gonna lawyer up."

"Maybe we should call Mr. D'Angelo right now."

Sam shook his head. "I don't want to bother Jimmy unless we have to."

"You're sure?"

"Yeah, they'll figure out who caused that explosion." Sam paused. "Or *somebody* will figure it out, anyway."

Phyllis frowned. She knew what he meant, and the fact that the cloud of suspicion above his head seemed to be thickening just gave her more incentive to dig into this case and uncover some answers. But he was putting all his faith in her, and that worried her. What if she let him down? What if the Rangers wound up arresting Sam? Even worse, what if he wound up indicted, tried, and convicted?

She wasn't sure she could live without Sam Fletcher anymore.

Phyllis swallowed. She was getting ahead of herself, and she knew it. There was no reason to indulge in wild speculation.

Thankfully, she was distracted from doing

so by Sam saying, "Hey, there's Carolyn and Eve."

Their friends were standing near the front of the tent. Phyllis and Sam made their way through the crowd to join them. Felicity, Josh, and Nick weren't with them, and as Phyllis and Sam came up, Phyllis asked, "What happened to the others?"

"That man Boudreau came along and latched on to Felicity," Carolyn said. "I don't know where they went."

"Probably for an interview," Sam said.

"Without a cameraman?" Carolyn pointed across the tent. "He made Josh and Nick go over there to the press area. I don't think an interview was what Boudreau had in mind."

"Well, maybe an off-the-record one."

The look Carolyn gave Sam showed just how much she believed that.

Eve said, "Hiram told us we could sit in the reserved section."

"You're on a first-name basis with him now?" Phyllis asked.

Eve smiled. "Of course."

"You're wasting your time," Carolyn said. "He's got his eye on Felicity, just like that Hammersmith man did."

"Experience and guile nearly always emerges triumphant in the end, dear."

Eve didn't even know that Hiram Boudreau had sold his company for at least ten million dollars a few years earlier. If she had, she might have been a little less lackadaisical about the man's interest in Felicity.

The first few rows of seating were marked off with bright yellow cord. It bore an uncomfortable resemblance to crime scene tape, Phyllis thought. The four of them sat down as more people continued to crowd into the tent and the noise level grew.

Phyllis looked around for Sergeant Culbertson or the other Texas Ranger and didn't see either of them. She felt confident both of them were around somewhere, though, probably close by. She saw half a dozen other security officers in addition to Ken. As big as the crowd was, that didn't really seem like enough, but so far everyone was being well-behaved and as long as they stayed that way, everything would be fine.

Hiram Boudreau suddenly appeared near the bandstand, carrying a cordless microphone. With an agility that belied his age, he jumped up onto the platform. Shadows had started to gather underneath the tent, but they were dispelled instantly as lights attached to the support poles came on. Boudreau lifted the microphone to his mouth, and an audible click signaled that he had turned it on. A burst of feedback made him lower it again without saying anything. The shrill squeal served to get everyone's attention, though, and make the crowd in the tent quiet down.

Boudreau tried again with the mike and this time didn't cause any feedback. He waved his other hand above his head as he greeted the crowd by saying, "Howdy, howdy, howdy! And welcome to the Great Chili Cook-Off!"

Applause, shouts, and enthusiastic whistles came in response. Boudreau let the tumult die down, then continued, "I want to thank each and every one of you for bein' here and making this get-together the biggest and best celebration of chili aficionados in the world!"

That bought more rowdy applause. A lot of these people had been drinking all day, Phyllis thought, so there was a good chance they would interrupt Boudreau's welcoming remarks every time he paused to take a breath.

"For those of you who don't know me, I'm Hiram Boudreau —"

More cheers and whoops.

"Owner, mayor, and Grand High Poobah of Cactus Bluff, Texas!"

The crowd just about raised the roof off the tent for that one.

"Also, founder and chief judge of the Great Chili Cook-Off, the most prestigious chili-cookin' competition in the world!"

This time, Phyllis thought she felt the ground shake a little.

Boudreau hadn't exactly dressed up for the ceremony, she noticed. He wore combat boots, another pair of cut-off jeans that prominently displayed his scabby knees, a psychedelic tie-dyed T-shirt that screamed 1967, and what appeared to be the same camo cap he had sported the previous night when he was putting on his impromptu dance performance.

He took off that cap now and held it over his heart as a solemn expression appeared on his face. "As I reckon all of y'all know by now, one of the most beloved of our contestants met an untimely end this morning when Joe D. Hammersmith went to that great chili pot in the sky."

A few scattered boos rang out.

"Here now!" Boudreau scolded. "That's no way to act. Have some respect for the dead, folks. I know ol' Joe D. rubbed a few folks the wrong way from time to time, but he was still one of us. And he was the three-time defendin' grand champion of the cook-off. That ought to be worth a moment of silence, and that's what I'm calling for right now, in honor of Joe D. Hammersmith."

Still holding his cap over his heart, Boudreau closed his eyes, bowed his head, and lowered the microphone to his side. Although it took a few seconds for the noise to fade away, the people gathered in the tent gradually complied with his call for a moment of silence. A hush settled over the crowd. Some of them — perhaps even many of them, Phyllis thought, recalling how Hammersmith had seemed to be widely disliked — might regard themselves as hypocrites for going along with this display, but she didn't see it that way. Hammersmith had been a human being, after all, and his life had ended suddenly and painfully, probably deliberately, and there was something awful about that.

"All right," Boudreau said when the silence had dragged out long enough, before it became too awkward, "let's get on with it." He tugged his cap down on his head again. "That's what Joe D. would've wanted us to do. Nobody enjoyed these little get-togethers of ours more than he did. He told me himself what a great time he always had here and how he looked forward all year to his trip to Cactus Bluff every summer. So the best way for us to honor ol' Joe D.'s memory is to have ourselves one hell of a blow-out!"

That gave the crowd an excuse for another frenzied response. Boudreau did a little jig back and forth across the bandstand that urged them on. People began a rhythmic clapping as Boudreau threw himself into the dance. He had urged the crowd not to let Hammersmith's death ruin their fun, and it certainly appeared that he intended to follow his own advice.

Eve leaned close to Phyllis to be heard over the commotion and said, "I hope Hiram remembers that ticker of his and doesn't push himself too hard!"

Boudreau didn't seem to be in any distress. He wasn't even breathing very hard when he finally stopped dancing and held up both arms to call for the crowd to quiet down again.

"Now, we all aim to have a lot of fun this weekend —"

More whooping.

"But y'all know the real reason we're here, and it's serious business." Boudreau paused, looked to his right, then to his left, then addressed the crowd again. "It's chili!"

Wild applause greeted that declaration.

"The best chili cooks in the whole wide world are right here under this big ol' tent tonight, folks," he continued when he could be heard again. "And they'll be workin' their culinary magic all weekend to whip up the best-tastin' chili you'll ever find anywhere!" He reached in the hip pocket of his cut-offs and pulled out a folded piece of paper. "I've got here a list of all the people who are entered in the competition. When I call your name, I want you to stand up and wave to the crowd, if you're sittin' down. If you're already on your feet, find some other way to let us know where you are. Hold your applause to the end, folks, otherwise we're liable to be here all night, and then you won't get to dance to the music of all the great bands we got lined up to play for you tonight! Here we go! Rusty Abernathy! Tom Allen! Jordan Anderson!"

Despite what Boudreau had said about the audience holding its applause, there were a few scattered claps and shouts of encouragement each time he called out a name from the list in his hand. Even with that, the announcement of the contestants went fairly quickly.

When Boudreau got to Sam's name, Sam stood up, turned to face the crowd, and gave a brief, self-conscious wave. Phyllis knew he wasn't accustomed to being the center of attention and didn't particularly care for the sensation.

Carolyn said, "I'll bet he's not going to read the names of everyone who entered the other contests." Earlier in the day, she had gone to the office tent and signed up for both the side dish and the leftovers contests.

"Well, chili's sort of the main event in this competition," Sam said. "I don't think he's tryin' to slight anybody."

"It just seems to me that people are a little fanatical about it."

Phyllis said, "I think passionate is a better word."

"So do I," Eve said.

When Boudreau was finished with the list of contestants and there had been a long, thunderous round of applause for all of them, he said, "Now, we've got some mighty fine entertainment tonight for your boot-scootin' pleasure, and first up are my friends B.J. Sawyer and the Lavaca River Boys! So give 'em a great big Cactus Bluff welcome and then get on up and dance!"

The four musicians Phyllis and her friends had seen the previous night came up onto the bandstand carrying their instruments. One of them set up microphones, and then they launched into a cover of "All My Exes Live in Texas" that soon had a lot of the crowd dancing.

Having grown up a Baptist in Texas in the middle of the Twentieth Century, Phyllis didn't dance, although she didn't disapprove of anyone who wanted to do so. She enjoyed all kinds of music, so the hand-clapping, toe-tapping country tunes played by the band from Hallettsville were fine. After a while, though, she began to get a little tired, so she said to Sam, "I think I'll go back to the trailer."

"I'll walk you," he replied without hesitation.

Phyllis was about to tell him that wasn't necessary, but when she glanced outside the tent she saw that full night had fallen, and although everything around here was fairly brightly lit, she didn't mind admitting that some company would be welcome.

Eve wasn't ready to leave, however, so Carolyn said, "I'll stay for a while longer and then the two of us will walk back together."

"That's fine with me," Eve said, "unless I get a better offer."

"Do you ever stop?"

"I will one of these days," Eve said. "When I get old."

As they were leaving the tent, Phyllis said to Sam, "Are you sure you don't mind? I could tell you were enjoying yourself."

"I like that good old country music, but I like spendin' time with you even more. I'm fine with leavin'." He chuckled. "Anyway, I need to get a good night's sleep. I've got a big day of chili cookin' comin' up tomorrow."

As they started back toward the rows of motor homes and travel trailers, Phyllis once again took note of the constable's Jeep. This time it was parked over by the smaller office tent, and someone was standing beside it. At first she figured it was Chuck Snyder, but then the shape parted and became two, then merged into one again.

A couple of people were necking over there, she thought, using the old-fashioned word out of habit because it hadn't been old-fashioned when she had learned it. In fact, when she'd learned about necking, she had been young herself, or at least young compared to the age she was now. She felt her cheeks warming. Everything she had done back in those days would seem tamer than tame to the young people of today, but she had fond memories of that time anyway. She took Sam's hand and squeezed it, and he squeezed back.

She might have allowed herself to drift farther into those pleasant reminiscences, if

at that moment a car hadn't turned somewhere in the distance and swept twin head-
light beams through the encampment. The
illumination was a mere flash across the
couple beside the Jeep . . .

But it was enough for Phyllis to recognize
them. That was Constable Chuck Snyder
beside his official vehicle, all right.

But the person in his arms with her mouth
pressed to his was McKayla Carson.

CHAPTER 14

Chuck was facing Phyllis and Sam as he stood by the Jeep, and in that brief moment of illumination he must have spotted them a few yards away. He broke the kiss, pushed McKayla away, stepped around her, and came toward the two of them, one hand lifted and held out in front of him.

"Mrs. Newsom, Mr. Fletcher, wait. This isn't —"

"Isn't what it looks like?" Sam said. As he went on, Phyllis knew he had seen the same thing she had. "Looked to me like you were makin' out with a girl young enough to be your, well, your little sister, I reckon. You gonna try to tell me that's not what was goin' on?"

In the shadows, Phyllis couldn't see Chuck's face that well, but he made little movements that seemed jerky and agitated and his voice was strained as he said, "That's not exactly the way it happened.

McKayla caught me by surprise —"

"Like a kissin' ninja?"

Chuck scrubbed a hand over his face in a frustrated gesture. "I didn't kiss her. She kissed me. I didn't encourage her —"

Coolly, McKayla said, "I'm standing right here, you know. And you certainly didn't *dis*courage me, Chuck. You know this is what you wanted. We've both wanted it for a long time."

"No! I mean —"

"I've seen the way you look at me. I know how you feel about me." She stepped closer to him and rested a hand on his chest. "I feel the same way. We were meant to be together."

Chuck shook his head and tried to put some distance between them again, but when he moved back McKayla went with him. Her head was tipped back so she could stare up at him adoringly.

Somewhat to Phyllis's surprise, she was starting to find herself believing what the young constable had said, to a certain extent, anyway. McKayla seemed to have a crush on him, and it was possible she had initiated this romantic encounter, probably taking him by surprise as he claimed. However, Chuck hadn't been struggling to get out of her embrace, and in fact his arms had been around her, too. She might have thrown herself at him, but he hadn't pushed her away . . . until they'd been caught.

Now he said, "Look, McKayla, this is all wrong. You need to go on back to the concert. You shouldn't have followed me out here —"

"Why not? Why shouldn't the two of us be together if that's what we want?"

"Because I'm ten years older than you! And your dad —"

"Are you afraid of him? I'll make him understand how this is the right thing for both of us."

"But it's not," Chuck argued. "You need to find some guy your own age —"

"In *Cactus Bluff*?" McKayla's tone made it obvious how unlikely she considered that possibility to be. "Except for this one weekend out of the year, you and I are the only people around here under the age of fifty!" Anger crept into her voice as she went on, "Or maybe you want me to fool around with one of those old geezers like Mr. Hammersmith. He didn't care how old I am!"

Before Chuck could react to that, someone not too far away called, "McKayla! McKayla, are you out here?"

Phyllis recognized the voice of Wendell

169

Carson, the girl's father. Chuck obviously did, too, because she heard an obvious gulp come from him.

McKayla called sweetly, "Over here, Daddy."

With a note of desperation in his voice, Chuck said, "Please, Mrs. Newsom, Mr. Fletcher, don't say anything. We can work all this out —"

"Goes a little against the grain, son," Sam said, "but I suppose I can give you the benefit of the doubt . . . for now."

"So can I," Phyllis said.

Wendell Carson strode up out of the shadows. With the four of them standing there, apparently talking, the situation looked a lot more innocent than it had a few minutes earlier. Carson peered at Sam and Phyllis and said, "Who's there?"

"Sam Fletcher, Mr. Carson." Sam stuck his hand out. "We met earlier today. I'm one of the contestants."

"Oh, yeah, sure." Carson shook hands with him. "Good to see you again." He turned to his daughter. "McKayla, what are you doing out here. I missed you at the concert."

"Mrs. Newsom and Mr. Fletcher were going back to their trailer," McKayla replied without missing a beat. "I thought I'd walk

170

with them and make sure they got there all right. You know how easy it is to get turned around out here, Daddy, especially in the dark. We ran into Constable Snyder along the way."

"Oh. Well, that was nice of you to help these folks."

Carson had swallowed his daughter's lie completely, Phyllis thought. And that falsehood had sprung to McKayla's lips quite easily. Clearly, she wasn't the sweet, innocent teenager she had seemed to be at first.

But then, Phyllis had taught junior high long enough to know that most teenagers weren't all that sweet and innocent.

Carson went on, "When I saw you, Constable, I was afraid there'd been some more trouble. After what happened this morning, everybody's a little nervous, I guess. I'll feel better about things once the Rangers decide that explosion was just an accident. Shoot, that's bad enough all by itself."

"Yeah, you're right," Chuck said. "It was a real tragedy."

"Well, I don't know that I'd go so far as to say *that* —" Carson stopped what he was saying with a shake of his head. "Shouldn't speak ill of the dead, I suppose. I don't mind admitting, though, that Joe D. Hammersmith always rubbed me the wrong way. Still, I wouldn't wish for anybody to blow up like that."

Carson knew that Hammersmith had made a pass at McKayla, Phyllis recalled. And Carson, though now a judge in the competition, had been one of the contestants in the past, so he had to know quite a bit about propane grills. Enough to sabotage one and cause it to explode? A doting father might feel justified in doing that if he thought he was protecting his daughter.

Something else was stirring in Phyllis's mind, though. Although Hammersmith had been the only victim of the explosion, a blast like that easily could have injured or even killed someone else. All it would have taken was for somebody to be in the wrong place at the wrong time . . . A killer would have to be pretty callous to risk that, and somehow, Wendell Carson just didn't strike Phyllis as that type.

Still, there was no evidence to let her rule him out entirely as a suspect. Since no one knew exactly when the sabotage had taken place — although almost certainly sometime during the night — it would be difficult for anyone to pin down an alibi.

Carson put a hand on McKayla's shoulder and continued, "Why don't you come on back to the concert with me? I'm sure the constable can help these folks get where they're going, if they need a hand."

"Actually, we're fine," Phyllis said. "Aren't we, Sam?"

"Yep," he said. He pointed and added, "The War Wagon's right over there."

"Is that what you call your trailer?" Carson asked. "I remember that movie! It's a good one."

"You bet."

Carson had hold of McKayla's arm by now. "Come on, honey," he said as he steered her away from the others. "Good night, folks. See you tomorrow."

McKayla cast a glance toward Chuck, who just smiled weakly and then turned his head away. Phyllis could see the girl's face well enough to read the angry expression that passed briefly over it. McKayla had been waiting for Chuck to speak up and declare their love for each other. She was going to have a long wait for that, Phyllis thought.

When the Carsons were gone, Chuck leaned back against the fender of his Jeep and heaved a shaky sigh. "Thank you for not saying anything," he told Phyllis and Sam. "I swear to you I never intended for that to happen —"

"You don't have to explain," Sam said.

"Both of us used to teach school. I've seen plenty of teenage girls who flirted with their male teachers. Sometimes they even got serious about it. I'm sure some of those fellas were tempted, too, but a man's got to know there are some lines he can't cross."

"I do, I promise you I do. She just took me by surprise . . ." Chuck's voice trailed off as he shook his head. "But that's no excuse, is it? You're right, I, uh, didn't react as quickly as I should have . . ."

Phyllis said, "If I were you, I'd be careful about being alone around that young woman in the future."

"I intend to, Mrs. Newsom. I can promise you that." Chuck paused, then went on, "I can count on both of you not to spread any rumors . . . ?"

"We're not gossips," Sam said. "You take care of your business, and we'll take care of ours."

"And speaking of business," Phyllis said, "have the Rangers talked to you about how their investigation is going?"

Chuck didn't say anything for a moment. When he did, Phyllis could almost see his forehead creasing in a frown, even though the gloom obscured such details. "Are you asking me about an official investigation, Mrs. Newsom?"

"I just thought Sergeant Culbertson or the other Ranger might have mentioned whether Mr. Hammersmith's death has been ruled a homicide."

"And you want to know because . . . ?"

"Curiosity."

Again Chuck hesitated before answering, "As a matter of fact, I can't tell you anything official because I don't know anything. The Rangers talk to the sheriff's department, not me. I'm just a local constable. I guess it didn't occur to them to keep me in the loop. From the way they're acting, though, it seems to me like they're treating it as a murder."

Phyllis thought the same thing. She said, "It seems to me that they ought to be asking for your help. They may have the forensic resources, but you know these people. You must have grown up around here."

"My dad has a ranch south of here," Chuck admitted. "But how did you know that?"

"Usually, young people don't move *into* an area like this. When they move, they move out to a bigger town. I figured you must have ties in the area, or you wouldn't still be here."

"I like it here," Chuck said. "I still help out some on the ranch, but I wasn't cut out for doing that all the time like my brothers are. I was always more interested in law enforcement. It just seemed like the right thing to me, you know."

"My son is a deputy for the sheriff's department back home," Phyllis said. "So I know exactly what you mean."

"I'd like to do that, too, someday, or even be a Ranger. So you can understand why I don't want this McKayla thing to get blown all out of proportion."

Sam said, "How it gets regarded is up to you, son. Keep your distance from her and I reckon you don't have to worry."

"That's exactly what I plan on doing. But you don't know how stubborn she can be."

"Doesn't matter. You're the grown-up here."

Chuck nodded, then said, "I was making a regular patrol when McKayla followed me out here, but now I'd better get back over to the concert. There's been enough drinking going on today that things could get out of hand. Although to be honest, they're less likely to tonight."

"Because Joe D. Hammersmith is dead?" Phyllis said.

"Well, yeah. Trouble seemed to follow that guy around. But what happened to him, that's got folks sobered up, at least a little

compared to the way it usually is."

Chuck told them good night and walked off toward the big tent. Phyllis didn't try to stop him, and neither did Sam. Once the constable was gone, however, Sam chuckled and said, "I thought you were about to blackmail that poor young fella into helpin' you investigate Hammersmith's murder."

"Do you really think I'd do that?"

"Once you get on the trail of something, it's sort of hard to get you off of it."

"Like a bloodhound, you mean?"

Sam laughed again and said, "Don't go puttin' words in my mouth." His tone grew more solemn as they started walking toward the trailer. "Maybe I was a little too hard on ol' Chuck. You've got to admit, that girl *looks* like she's of age. When we first met her, we all figured she was in her twenties."

"Did any of your students ever have a crush on you?"

"I couldn't tell you. I don't know. I never thought about things like that. I just concentrated on doin' my job."

"I'm sure they did," Phyllis said.

"Maybe so, but you couldn't prove it by me."

After a moment, she said, "What do you think about Wendell Carson?"

"You mean, would he blow up Hammersmith because the fella got fresh with Mc-Kayla?" Sam shook his head. "I don't think so. He might punch the son of a gun — in fact, I'd bet on it — but riggin' up an explosion like that doesn't seem like somethin' he would do."

"I agree," Phyllis said. "And yet, I'm sure he's been around a lot of propane grills in the past. He would have had the knowledge to do it. That's means, motive, and considering that we don't know when the sabotage was carried out, he could have had the opportunity, too."

"If he was involved with the blast, I reckon the Rangers will figure it out."

"Will they? Or are they going to be too busy trying to come up with the evidence to convict someone else?"

"Like me? We both know I didn't kill Hammersmith. They can't convict an innocent man."

Phyllis said, "It happens all the time, Sam. You know that as well as I do. You've seen how some of those cases we've been mixed up in have almost resulted in a great injustice."

"But they didn't . . . thanks to you." Sam stopped and nodded to the trailer. "Here we are. Want me to come in with you for a minute to make sure everything's all right?"

"Why wouldn't it be?"

"Can't ever tell," Sam said. "There's a killer on the loose, and if he knows that you're after him, he might think it'd be better not to let you get on his trail in the first place."

"You don't think . . . surely not . . . but I guess if you don't mind . . ."

"Let me go in and take a look around first. Won't take long. The War Wagon's not big enough to hide much."

Phyllis gave Sam the key. He unlocked the trailer's door and went inside, turning on the lights as he did so. After a surprisingly tense few seconds, he reappeared and told Phyllis, "All clear. Everything looks just like it did when we left."

"When you turned the lights on, it occurred to me that the killer might have arranged another explosion tied somehow to that switch. I was a little nervous."

"Huh," Sam said. "I'm sort of glad I didn't think of that, or I might have been worried, too. Well, you know what they say about the triumph of the uncluttered mind." He drew Phyllis into his arms, held her for a moment, and kissed the top of her head. "I'll see you in the mornin'. Get a good night's sleep."

"You, too," she told him. "Tomorrow's going to be a big day."

CHAPTER 15

Saturday, the first day of the competition, dawned bright and clear, which was no surprise because in this part of Texas it was almost always bright and clear. The temperature would be brutally hot before the day was over because the thin, dry atmosphere warmed quickly and easily.

The smell of smoked meat filled the air as Phyllis, Carolyn, and Eve stepped out of the trailer. Sam was already there with a pot of chili just starting to simmer on his grill. He smiled and said, "Mornin', ladies. Everything quiet last night?"

"Hardly," Carolyn said. "We could hear that music coming from the tent until the wee hours of the morning. I was beginning to think it would never stop and let us get some sleep."

"It didn't bother me," Eve said. "But I was worn out from dancing, I suppose."

"You should have been. It made me tired

just watching the way those old men kept flocking around you."

"I can't help it if I'm just naturally vivacious. Men respond to that." Eve laughed. "Hiram certainly did."

"You danced with Mr. Boudreau?" Phyllis asked.

"He's quite a charming gentleman. And my, does he love to dance. He has bad knees, but you'd never know it from watching him."

Sam said, "Yeah, I've never seen a fella break into a jig quite as easy as he does."

"Yes, but I was close enough to him to see him wince every now and then when he took a step," Eve said. "However, that didn't slow him down."

Carolyn stepped over to the grill and looked into the pot of chili. "This is starting to smell good," she told Sam. "I appreciate you letting me use your leftovers from yesterday for my recipes."

"Glad to do it," Sam told her.

"How does the judging work?" Phyllis asked.

"The judges will come around this afternoon and sample everybody's chili," Sam explained. "Then they'll pick the top twenty to compete again tomorrow, in the big tent. I'm hopin' I'll be one of 'em."

"I'm sure you will be," Phyllis said.

"Somebody'll be by in a little while to check the cookin' set-up and make sure everything's legal," Sam went on. "Other than that, it won't be very excitin'. Won't be much goin' on except for me stirrin' the pot and tastin' the chili every now and then and addin' spices. I'll have to keep an eye on the pot all day, though, to make sure nobody messes with it." He shook his head. "Chili cookin' is a cutthroat game."

"We can give you a hand if need be," Phyllis said. "In the meantime, I'll bring you some coffee and something to eat. I have muffins cooking right now."

A grin appeared on Sam's face. "Now that sounds mighty good," he said. "I can't let you take over for me. I'd get disqualified if someone else was mindin' the pot, but the food and coffee will be much appreciated. I'm gonna need fortifyin' throughout the day."

"We'll see to it that you don't starve," Phyllis said dryly.

When Phyllis took Sam's breakfast outside, she brought along a small plate of mini muffins and a cup of coffee for herself, too, and sat in the other lawn chair to eat with him. While they were doing that, Sam nodded toward town and said, "Here come our young friends."

He was talking about Felicity and Josh, Phyllis saw. Felicity looked ready to go on camera, as usual, and there was a good reason for that. She already had been.

"The sheriff's department just held a press briefing," Felicity announced without any greeting. "Joe D. Hammersmith's death has been ruled a homicide. Federal investigators from the Bureau of Alcohol, Tobacco, Firearms, and Explosives will be coming in later today. If this wasn't a big story before, it is now. You know what that means. There's going to be a lot of pressure for an arrest, and the sooner the better."

Phyllis thought about that fingerprint the Rangers had gotten from the piece of Hammersmith's grill they had recovered. Sergeant Culbertson didn't seem like the sort of man who would be stampeded into anything, but Phyllis also knew about the inherent rivalry between law enforcement agencies. That attitude was just made worse when federal authorities were involved. In a state as independent-minded as Texas, the Rangers wouldn't take kindly to the Feds sticking their noses in.

One way to forestall that would be to make an arrest before the BATFE even arrived on the scene.

That thought made Phyllis glance at Sam. He didn't seem concerned, but she certainly felt some unease stirring inside her.

The feeling was accompanied by a nagging sense that she had seen or heard something significant, something that hadn't quite lodged in her brain. At least, not where she could drag it into the open, examine it, and figure out what it meant. And even if she did, there were still too many things she didn't know. She needed more facts in order to move them around, piece them together, and form them into a picture that made sense.

Today might be a good day to ferret out some of those facts, she decided, since it didn't appear that much else would be going on.

She didn't want Felicity and Josh tagging along, though, but as Felicity asked, "What are you going to do about this, Mrs. Newsom?" she knew it might be difficult to shake them.

"Nothing right now," Phyllis answered. "Between the Rangers and the Federal agents, I'm not sure there's anything I *can* do. They'll have the investigation locked up tight."

"What sort of attitude is that?" Felicity demanded. "You've never hesitated to get right in there and mix it up with the law on those other cases."

"That's caused problems more than once, too," Phyllis pointed out.

"Don't tell me you're scared. You've never backed down from going after a killer before. Anyway . . . you're working for *Inside Beat,* remember?"

"I don't recall us ever negotiatin' a salary," Sam said. "I sort of had the feelin' we were unpaid interns, like ol' Josh here used to be."

"It was valuable experience," Josh said. "I wouldn't be where I am today without it."

Carolyn looked like she wanted to say something, Phyllis noticed, probably about how Josh's current position as Felicity's "producer" wasn't really that enviable, but she held it in.

"Well, if you're not going to get to the bottom of this, I may have to," Felicity said. "I'll go talk to those Rangers. I'm sure I can get something out of them."

Phyllis suspected that Felicity's charms wouldn't be worth much against Sergeant Culbertson's discretion and devotion to duty, but she didn't say anything. Briefly, she considered suggesting that the reporter talk to Constable Chuck Snyder instead, since Chuck seemed to be vulnerable to attractive young women, but she wasn't one to stir up unnecessary trouble.

"If I do think of anything that might be helpful, I'll let you know," she promised.

"All right," Felicity said with grudging acceptance. "You've got Josh's number?"

"Yes, I do."

"All right." Felicity gestured to Josh. "Come on, let's find those Rangers."

As the two of them walked off, Sam said quietly, "She's not gonna have any luck pryin' anything out of those fellas. Might as well butt up against a stone wall."

"She's determined, though." Phyllis smiled. "And it'll keep her busy."

"So that she won't get in your hair while you're trying to find the truth," Carolyn said. "I knew what you were doing."

Phyllis just shrugged a little. "I thought I might walk around and ask some questions here and there."

Sam leaned forward in his chair and said, "Dang it, you shouldn't be doin' that without me along. If you start closin' in on whoever killed Hammersmith, it could get dangerous. And I have to stay here and watch my chili!"

"I think I'm a long way from closing in on anybody," Phyllis said. "Anyway, it's broad daylight, and there are hundreds of people around. Nobody's going to try anything in a situation like that."

"Not unless they're desperate enough."

"Why don't I go with Phyllis?" Eve suggested. "I think we'd make a pretty formidable team. "Carolyn has to stay here to mess with her recipes, and she can make sure Sam doesn't need anything."

Carolyn frowned. Phyllis knew she didn't care for the way Eve had phrased that about "messing with her recipes", but Carolyn must have decided it wasn't worth arguing about because she didn't say anything — other than a faint "Hmmph."

"That sounds like a good idea," Phyllis agreed. "Let me finish my coffee and put on some better shoes for walking around."

"And I'll go get ready," Eve said. "I want to look my best, you know. There's no telling who we'll be talking to."

In other words, she wanted to impress any eligible bachelors they came across, Phyllis thought. Eve was definitely back to her old self, although Phyllis knew some of that was just an act, a way of protecting herself from brooding about her terrible track record with men.

Or as Eve might put it . . . fifth time's the charm.

The encampment seemed slightly subdued this morning, even though all the chili cooks were up and about and had their pots of red simmering. The concert, the drinking and dancing and celebrating, and the late hours of the previous night all combined to take a toll. Hangovers were bound to be running rampant this morning, Phyllis thought as she and Eve strolled along, and anyone who could sleep in probably was doing so.

They passed Kurt Middleton's motor home and found the man bending over a pot of chili, studying it as intently as if he could *see* whether it was good or not. Dark beard stubble covered his lean jaws, and his eyes were sunken more than usual in their sockets. They were a little bloodshot, too, Phyllis noticed.

"Good morning, Mr. Middleton," she said as she and Eve paused.

He straightened up from his scrutiny of the chili in the pot. "Do I know you?" he asked with a frown.

"I don't think we've been introduced. My name is Phyllis Newsom. This is my friend Eve Turner."

Middleton just grunted, clearly not impressed. "You're not in the contest, are you?" His tone implied that anyone who wasn't cooking chili today wasn't worth talking to.

"No, but my friend is. Sam Fletcher." Phyllis pointed. "Back over there."

"Yeah, I've seen him around." Middleton's frown deepened. "You were here the other night when I tangled with Hammersmith."

"That's right."

"He had it coming, you know," Middleton said. "They tell you not to speak ill of the dead, but sometimes that's what they deserve. Hammersmith broke up more than one marriage. He did his best to break up mine . . . and then he would have dumped Lindy and laughed about it. I don't know why she can't see that."

"So you're not upset about him being killed in that explosion?"

"I didn't say that," Middleton replied quickly. "There's talk that he was murdered, that somebody deliberately caused that blast. Let's be honest, I don't care all that much about Hammersmith, but with an explosion like that, somebody else could have been hurt."

Phyllis nodded solemnly and said, "I've thought the same thing."

Middleton rubbed at his nose with the back of his hand. "Propane's nothing to mess with if you don't know what you're doing. All it takes is a little leak, you know? The stuff's heavier than air, so if it's leaking it'll settle down on the ground, almost like a pool of water, you know. Then all it takes is a spark to set it off. I've seen grills blow up more than once because of something like that. Saw a guy killed once because of it, too."

"You mean it was a big explosion like the one that killed Mr. Hammersmith?"

"Well, actually, no, it wasn't that big. But it blew a meat fork right into a guy's throat. Speared him just like gigging a frog." Middleton shook his head. "Hell of a thing."

Eve shuddered a little and said, "How horrible."

"Yeah, it was. Hammersmith was lucky in a way. At least he went quick."

Phyllis didn't think Hammersmith would have regarded that as lucky. Either way, he wound up dead.

Nobody could count on a meat fork to fly in just the right direction to spear the intended victim. So the blast had to be big enough to kill Hammersmith by itself, she thought. She frowned slightly as she looked at Kurt Middleton's cooking set-up.

"You're several yards away from your motor home," she said. Now that she thought about it, Sam had placed his grill so that there was some distance between it and the War Wagon.

"Safety precaution. I'm around on the other side from where the ASME tank is located, too."

Eve said, "The what?"

"The propane tank that's built into the frame of the motor home. The letters stand for American Society of Mechanical Engineers." Middleton's tone was a little scornful as he added, "You're not an experienced RVer, are you?"

"This is the first time I've ever stayed in one," Eve admitted.

Middleton lost some of his truculent attitude. Like most men, he enjoyed explaining things. He pointed and said, "The tank's around on the other side. It holds 100 pounds of propane, and I'll use just about all of it this weekend."

Phyllis said, "But you set up your grill on this side so in case there's a fire or something, it won't set off the gas in the tank attached to the motor home."

"You got it, lady. It's just common sense."

"Yes, I can see that," Phyllis said, nodding. "Thank you, Mr. Middleton. I'd wish you luck in the contest, but since my friend is competing . . ."

"That's all right. I don't need luck. All I need is the best chili, and I've got that."

As Phyllis and Eve walked on, Phyllis recalled the things Jeff Porter had said to her the night before. Porter had been supremely confident that his chili was going to win the cook-off, too. Maybe that confidence, bordering on arrogance, was a requirement for such contests. If that was the case, Sam might not stand a chance, since he didn't have an arrogant bone in his body.

"That man thought you were just chatting with him," Eve said, "but those questions about the propane tank, there was a reason for those, wasn't there?"

"Something's not right about the set-up," Phyllis said. "The theory was that something caused Hammersmith's grill to explode, which set off the propane tank on his motor home, which made the gasoline tank explode as well. But Hammersmith had been entering these chili cook-offs for years. Would he have set up his grill in a place where that could happen?"

"I'm sure I don't know. And since it's all burned up, how would you ever find out?"

"I can think of someone who might know," Phyllis replied, remembering how Sam had admitted to looking at Joe D. Hammersmith's grill two nights earlier. She would have to talk to him later and find out just how many details he recalled.

"If it wasn't the grill that caused the explosion, what do you believe did?"

Phyllis shook her head and said, "I don't know enough at this point to have any sort of theory. But something's been bothering me, and I just can't figure out what it is."

"You'll figure it out. You always —"

Eve stopped short and let out a surprised little yelp. Someone had come up silently behind her and grabbed her.

CHAPTER 16

"Good mornin', darlin'," Hiram Boudreau said. "Is it too early for some more dancin'?"

Eve laughed and said, "Let go of me, you crazy man. Didn't you get enough dancing last night?"

"How could any man ever get enough of cavortin' around with a pretty girl in his arms?" Boudreau asked as a grin stretched across his bearded face. He let go of Eve and stepped back. "But say, where are you ladies headed on this fine, beautiful mornin'?"

"No place in particular," Phyllis said. "We're just taking a walk."

"I'll invite myself along, then." Boudreau chuckled. "It's my town, after all."

"I've been wondering about that. How in the world did you wind up owning an entire town?"

Phyllis already knew some of the answer to that, but she wanted to find out what

Boudreau would say.

"Oh, I reckon it was just a whim. I've always been a mite on the impulsive side. Used to be an oil wildcatter, you know, and in that game, you learn to follow your hunches."

Eve said, "You were an oilman?"

"Yes'm, I sure was, for a whole heap of years. Tramped all over every square foot of West Texas, so I'd been in these parts before and remembered that I liked it here. After I retired, it was natural to start thinkin' about movin' here. When I drove in and saw that practically every piece of property in town was for sale, that gave me the idea of buyin' the whole town. The folks who weren't already tryin' to sell their places jumped at my offers. So I wound up bein' —"

"The Grand High Poobah of Cactus Bluff," Phyllis finished for him, which brought a bray of laughter from Boudreau.

"Yes, ma'am, that's exactly what I am," he said.

"What made you think of having a chili cook-off?" Eve asked.

"Well, my first thought was to turn this place into a retirement and resort community. Even though I'd sold my oil company, when I got down here I found that I wasn't ready to just put my feet up and do nothin' all day. The real estate deals didn't go as well as I'd hoped, so I started lookin' around for something else to do. I saw how successful that other chili contest had been and thought I might like to do somethin' like that. I've always liked chili." Boudreau chuckled. "I started off the very first year callin' it the world's biggest and best chili cook-off. Figured it would be a good idea to stake my claim right off the bat."

Phyllis said, "Even though it wasn't the biggest and best."

"Yet," Boudreau said. "But if you say somethin' long enough and loud enough, folks start to believe it, and then it comes true." He waved his skinny arms to take in their surroundings as they reached the main road at the edge of downtown. "You can see for yourself how well that worked. This weekend, Cactus Bluff is the center of the chili world."

"You should certainly be proud," Eve said.

"Oh, I am, darlin', I am. This town and this contest, they're my babies." He took Eve's hand. "You sure I can't interest you in another dance?"

"But there's no music."

Boudreau put his hand on his chest and said, "I got the music right here in my heart."

Eve laughed and shook her head. "Go on with you. Maybe tonight. There'll be more performances then, won't there?"

"Yeah, folks'll be jammin' all over the camp. I'll look you up."

"It's a date," Eve agreed.

Boudreau smiled, waved, and shuffled off along the street, greeting pedestrians, shaking hands, slapping backs, and laughing.

"He's quite the colorful character, isn't he?" Eve said.

"He certainly is," Phyllis said. "Like a cross between Gabby Hayes and J.R. Ewing."

"And a former oilman, to boot. How much money do you think he made from selling his company?"

Phyllis had an idea about that from the research she had done, but she just shook her head and said, "I don't know." There was no point in egging Eve on by telling her that Boudreau had collected at least five million dollars from the sale of A/B Exploration. Maybe more than that, depending on what sort of partnership agreement he'd had with Harlan Anders.

Eve would never be happy living in an isolated place like Cactus Bluff, though, Phyllis knew, so it was better if she didn't even start thinking about marriage where

Hiram Boudreau was concerned.

Up ahead, a blond woman was looking at the Indian jewelry displayed at one of the stands set up for the weekend. She glanced around at Phyllis and Eve, smiled, and Phyllis recognized her as Julie Glennister.

"Good morning," Phyllis said. "I suppose your husband is hard at work cooking his chili right now."

Julie laughed and said, "Of course. Why else would we drive hundreds of miles out here in the middle of nowhere, all the way from Granbury? What could be more important than chili?"

Despite the laugh and the light tone of the woman's words, Phyllis heard a trace of resentment in Julie's response. She said, "It *is* a long way."

"It's all right, I suppose. Royce works hard, and cooking chili is really his only hobby. You wouldn't think it would be so time-consuming, though. And expensive. He has to have the newest, fanciest grill every year."

"Well, that probably helps in the contest," Phyllis said.

"You'd think so, wouldn't you? But he still couldn't manage to beat Joe D."

Phyllis said, "But Mr. Hammersmith cheated in the contest and pre-cooked his meat. At least that's what your husband said the other night."

"Hmmph. Royce always claimed that, but I think he was just trying to make himself feel better because Joe D. always came out ahead of him. It's easier to believe the other fellow is cheating than it is to accept that you're just not good enough." Julie paused, then added hastily, "I didn't mean that the way it sounded. Royce is a fine man."

"I'm sure he is."

"Anyway, with what he spends on this contest, I don't mind buying myself a few pretty things while we're here each year." Julie picked up the turquoise and silver bracelet she'd been looking at. "Like this."

Eve said, "It's beautiful."

Julie slipped the bracelet onto her wrist and nodded. "And it's going to be mine. Royce may not ever notice it, but I will."

Phyllis nodded. She and Eve moved on down the street while Julie went to pay for the bracelet.

"That woman is primed and ready to cheat on her husband," Eve commented quietly. "I recognize the signs."

Phyllis said, "I thought the same thing. There's no reason to think she actually *would* . . ."

"But the thought has crossed her mind.

You know it has. You could tell she resents the time and money her husband spends on this contest, and she doesn't like being dragged out here every year. *And* she thinks that after going to that much trouble, the least he could do is win."

"Instead he always lost to Hammersmith."

"Did you hear how she called him Joe D.?" Eve asked. "She didn't sound like she hated him, the way her husband does."

"Just because she didn't hate him doesn't mean she was involved with him."

"You're the detective, dear," Eve said. "Aren't you supposed to be suspicious of everybody?"

That was the problem. All the other cook-off contestants Phyllis had talked to since arriving in Cactus Bluff had had valid reasons to dislike Joe D. Hammersmith. There were scores of other contestants she *hadn't* talked to. Did all of them have motives for murder as well? How could she ever sort through them? That was a job for the authorities, but with the Rangers concentrating on Sam because of that fingerprint, would they take the time and trouble to canvass everyone else in town? Phyllis thought that was pretty unlikely, since they already had a piece of physical evidence.

Constable Chuck Snyder's Jeep was

parked at the sidewalk up ahead, in front of the market, but the young lawman wasn't in the vehicle. He came out of the building as Phyllis and Eve approached, though, and saw them walking toward him.

Phyllis saw alarm leap into Chuck's eyes, and for a moment he looked like he wanted to turn around and retreat back into the market rather than face them. With a visible squaring of his shoulders, though, he took a deep breath and continued striding toward the Jeep.

"Good morning, Constable," Phyllis greeted him as they all came to a stop on the sidewalk beside the Jeep.

"Morning, Mrs. Newsom," Chuck replied. He managed a smile and nod, then glanced at Eve. "Mrs. Turner, isn't it?"

"That's right," Eve said. "Hello, Deputy. I mean Constable." She returned the smile and shook her head. "I'm afraid I've always had a hard time keeping those things straight."

"That's all right. I'm definitely one rung lower than a deputy sheriff, though. At least."

Phyllis said, "The Rangers and the sheriff's department still aren't sharing any information about the case with you?"

Chuck had been casting wary glances

toward Phyllis, as if he were worried that she was going to bring up his encounter with McKayla she had witnessed the night before. Now her question made it appear that she didn't intend to embarrass him, and she saw him relax slightly.

Not too much, though, because the threat was still there, and he knew it. The fact that it was likely to make him more cooperative hadn't escaped Phyllis, either.

"Rangers don't share much information with anybody," Chuck said. "They're used to handling everything themselves when they're called in. The sheriff probably doesn't like that, but there's not much he can do about it."

Eve said, "They should be taking advantage of your skills, too. The important thing is solving the case, not who gets credit for it."

"That's the way it should work," Chuck said, "but we're not naïve enough to believe that it does, are we?"

Eve laughed and shook her head. "Not in the real world."

Phyllis said, "I've been thinking about how things were set up around Mr. Hammersmith's motor home. It seems to me —"

Before she could go on, someone behind her called, "Phyllis!" She turned and saw

Felicity Prosper hurrying toward her, followed by Josh as usual and this time by Nick Baker as well. Nick had his camera, as always.

Felicity was a little out of breath as she came up, but she recovered almost instantly and despite the heat, which was rising even though it was still a couple of hours until midday, she looked cool and elegant. She looked at Chuck and said, "Felicity Prosper from *Inside Beat*."

"Yes, ma'am, I know who you are," Chuck said.

"I'd like to get an official statement from you regarding the murder of Joe D. Hammersmith, Constable Snyder."

Chuck shook his head. "I'm afraid I can't make any such statement. I don't know any more than you do, Ms. Prosper."

"But you're a law enforcement officer —"

"I break up drunken fights and tell the people mixed up in them to cool off," Chuck interrupted her. Phyllis heard the frustration in his voice. "Normally I enforce the speed limit here in town, too, but with so many people in the road all the time, nobody driving can go any faster than a crawl."

"So you have no insights to offer into the murder?"

"None," Chuck said flatly.

Felicity glanced at Josh, who gestured for Nick to stop recording. She turned to Phyllis and said in an accusatory tone, "You were supposed to let me know before you did any investigating."

"I wasn't investigating," Phyllis said, even though that was exactly what she'd been doing. "Eve and I were just taking a walk and ran into Constable Snyder. We were chatting, that's all."

Felicity rolled her eyes as if she didn't believe that for a second. She said, "I need coffee."

"I'll go get some for you," Josh offered without hesitation.

Chuck pointed with a thumb toward the market. "You can get some in there. It's good, and it's a little closer than the café. But let's face it, nothing is very far away in Cactus Bluff. No matter where you are, you can turn around in a circle and see the whole town."

"I don't see how you stand to live here," Felicity said. "I'll get my own coffee. You didn't fix it right last time, Josh."

She walked across the parking lot toward the building, trailed by an apologizing Josh and the always impassive Nick. Chuck watched them go and shook his head a little.

"Is she always like that?"

"She has a good heart . . . I think," Phyllis said. "But she's beautiful and she's used to having the spotlight on her all the time. That has to have an effect on someone. Although I certainly wouldn't know from experience."

Chuck directed a curious frown toward her. "Why did she ask if you were investigating the murder? You're just . . . I mean, no offense, but . . ."

"Just a retired schoolteacher?" Eve said.

"Hey, I didn't even know that much," Chuck replied with a shrug.

"You won't ever get Phyllis to brag, but she's solved several murders in the past. She's famous back where we live."

"Notorious may be more like it," Phyllis said. "The local police and sheriff's department aren't too fond of me getting involved in their cases, and I'm sure it's the same here."

"But you're trying to find out who's responsible for the explosion that killed Hammersmith?"

"Well . . . the Rangers seem to have some idea that my friend Sam is involved, and I know that's not true."

"And the best way to prove that is to expose the real killer," Chuck mused. "That's . . . interesting."

"I'll say it is," Eve put in. "The two of you should work together."

Phyllis and Chuck looked at each other, and Phyllis knew they had both realized that wasn't such a bad idea.

CHAPTER 17

"The sheriff's department conducted the forensic investigation before the Rangers got here, didn't they?" Phyllis asked.

"That's right," Chuck replied with a nod.

"Is there any way you could get a look at it? Someone in the department who owes you a favor?"

For a moment, Chuck didn't answer as he gave Phyllis an intent look. Then he said, "You really are a detective, aren't you? You don't mind playing hardball."

"I told you," Eve said.

Unspoken between Phyllis and Chuck was the knowledge she and Sam held over his head. If Chuck had been telling the truth about the encounter with McKayla Carson, he hadn't really done much wrong. It wasn't his fault the girl had a crush on him. He could have reacted a little differently when she got aggressive with him, but he hadn't broken any laws.

Still, if people started gossiping about him and McKayla, it would be embarrassing and not good for his future as a law enforcement officer. More than likely, Phyllis would never go so far as to reveal what she knew about him . . . but he didn't know that.

"Sam and I have done some investigative work for a defense lawyer in Weatherford," Phyllis explained. "We've learned how to do what's necessary to protect our client."

"You don't have a client," Chuck pointed out.

"No, but Sam's the one in jeopardy this time, which makes me even more determined to find out the truth."

Chuck drew in a deep breath, sighed, and nodded. "I'll see what I can do," he said. "I have a few buddies in the department, guys I used to rodeo with when we were in school. I can't guarantee any of them will be willing to risk helping me, but they might. I'm going to need something in return, though."

Phyllis cocked an eyebrow. She had thought that keeping quiet about McKayla would be enough repayment for the favor.

"What do you mean, Constable?" she asked.

"If you figure out who caused that explosion, you tell me, not the Rangers or the sheriff's department."

Eve said, "You want the collar." When Chuck looked at her, she smiled and added, "I wrote a mystery novel."

He shrugged, turned back to Phyllis, and said, "Yes, I'd like to make the arrest if it's possible."

"I'll do what I can," she told him. "As you said, it's difficult to guarantee anything in a situation like this."

He shook his head, muttered, "I can't believe I'm doing this," and climbed into the Jeep. He promised Phyllis, "I'll talk to you later if I find out anything."

"So will I," she said.

Carefully, he pulled the Jeep away from the sidewalk and made a U-turn through the road, going slow to avoid the people crossing to the other side. As Eve watched him drive away, she said, "This could be just the break you need to crack the case wide-open."

"We'll see about that," Phyllis said. "I just hope the constable doesn't double-cross me."

"He won't. He strikes me as a trustworthy young man, and he needs your help as much as you need his."

They walked the rest of the way up one side of the street, then crossed over and went back down the other side. In a town the size of Cactus Bluff, that didn't take long, in spite of the crowds on the sidewalks and in the road itself. They didn't encounter anyone else Phyllis needed to talk to about the case, so they headed back toward the rows of motor homes and travel trailers. Phyllis wanted to talk to Sam about the idea that had occurred to her earlier.

What little breeze there was came from the direction of the encampment, and it carried with it the smell of dozens of pots of chili. That was indeed a mouth-watering blend of aromas. The hour was approaching noon, so Phyllis didn't know if she was getting hungry because of the time or if that sensation came from all the tempting smells in the air.

When they reached the War Wagon, Sam was sitting in one of the lawn chairs near the grill with his right ankle cocked on his left knee. He had a Western paperback in his hand. He grinned at Phyllis and Eve and said, "The chili's not ready yet. Of course, I figure you knew that."

From the open door of the travel trailer, Carolyn said, "Lunch just about is, though. I made chili with spicy cornbread waffles and some chili lasagna. There are still plenty of beans left over from yesterday, too, so I refried them, mixed them with leftover chili, and made chili topped hashbrown potato cakes. We won't go hungry as long as there's leftover chili!"

"And it's gonna last a while, I can promise you that," Sam added. "We'll be takin' quite a bit home with us."

Phyllis and Eve went inside, and Phyllis came back out a few minutes later with a glass of iced ginger citrus tea for herself and a glass for Sam. She handed it to him and sat down in the other lawn chair.

Sam took a big sip of the tea. "Oh, this is mighty good."

"It's a ginger citrus tea. I thought the ginger would give it a nice kick, and ginger is so healthy."

"It does have a nice taste to it."

"I did a little poking around while Eve and I were taking our walk," she said quietly. "We ran into Constable Snyder, and he's going to see if he can get his hands on a copy of the forensics report from the sheriff's department."

"Why would he do somethin' that risky?" Sam asked.

"Oh, he might have gotten the idea that it would be a good thing to help us, since we know about him and McKayla."

Sam laughed. "You've been around Jimmy

D'Angelo too much. He's like ol' Perry Mason. Doesn't mind bendin' the rules a little in order to see justice done."

"I'm not responsible for whatever ideas the constable might get in his head." Phyllis smiled. "But once Eve told him about those other cases I worked on, he didn't mind too much. I promised him that if I figured out this one, I'd share it with him first."

Sam nodded and said, "Sounds like a good deal to me. Both of you get something out of it. But what do you figure you'll find in that forensics report?"

Phyllis took a drink of her iced tea. In this heat, it tasted awfully good.

"I'm hoping it will say for sure whether the propane cylinder attached to Hammersmith's grill was the first thing to explode, the way we've assumed since it happened."

Sam frowned. "Why wouldn't it have been?"

Phyllis gestured at Sam's grill, then swept her hand toward the trailer. "You've allowed some distance between the grill and the trailer just in case of a fire, haven't you? And the grill is also positioned well away from the propane tank attached to the trailer."

"You been doin' research?"

"I happened to talk to Kurt Middleton

about propane safety."

"Middleton? The fella who punched out Hammersmith because he thought he was tryin' to steal his wife?"

"Yes, but we didn't discuss that today," Phyllis said.

"Well, you're right. I've got a twenty-pound cylinder on this grill, and if it was to blow up, it'd make a big old fireball and wreck the grill, for sure."

"But it wouldn't destroy the trailer, too."

Sam tugged at his earlobe, then scraped a thumbnail along his jaw as he considered what Phyllis had said. "Probably not."

"Would it set off the propane tank attached to the trailer?"

"I hope not. That's why I've got things set up like they are."

"And how was Hammersmith's grill set up?"

Sam leaned forward in his chair, everything else forgotten for the moment as he cast his mind back to the few minutes he had spent examining and admiring Joe D. Hammersmith's grill.

"Hammersmith was runnin' a Lydecker 6500," he said.

"That doesn't mean anything to me."

"It's top of the line," Sam explained. "Just a three-burner outfit, instead of a six, but with a computer in it so you can control the temperature down to a fraction of a degree."

"What size cylinder would he have in it?"

"Twenty, like mine, more than likely. That would be enough to last him through the competition unless somethin' unusual happened."

"And the one on his motor home? The ASME tank?"

That drew a chuckle from Sam. "You really have been studyin' this stuff, haven't you? That would be eighty or a hundred pounds, maybe even bigger."

"So if it blew up first, that would cause a large enough explosion to set off the motor home's gas tank, as well as the propane cylinder in the grill outside."

"It could sure work out that way," Sam allowed. "You think somebody sabotaged the tank on the motor home instead of on the grill?"

"I'm not sure what I think at this point," Phyllis said. "But the sequence of events everyone just assumed happened started seeming a little off to me. But as far as what actual difference it makes . . ." She shook her head. "I have no idea."

Lunch was wonderful. Phyllis tried all three of Carolyn's recipes using Sam's chili left over from the day before and found them all to be delicious. By the time she finished, her mouth burned a little from all the spices, but more iced tea took care of that.

As she and Sam were eating outside, she told him about the conversation with Julie Glennister. "She's a little different when she's away from her husband," Phyllis concluded. "She doesn't seem to care much for Royce's chili cooking hobby, and she was almost sympathetic to Hammersmith."

"You think she was messin' around with him?"

Phyllis thought about the question for a moment, then shook her head. "Honestly, I doubt it. But she might have been tempted, and Royce might have found out about it."

"I don't know. He doesn't seem like the type to blow somebody up."

"I agree. But we know from experience that you can never be absolutely certain how someone else is going to react."

"Shoot," Sam said, "half the time folks can't be sure how they're gonna react themselves until they find themselves in a bad situation. Everybody's capable of makin' a wrong decision."

Phyllis couldn't disagree with that. And murder was just about the worst decision of them all.

Carolyn had prepared samples of all the dishes she had cooked so that the judges could taste them, and after lunch she, Phyllis, and Eve carried the containers over to the big tent for the first round of the contest. Tables were set up for the food with numbered places for each entry on them. Carolyn found her spot and set out the containers, leaving them closed until the judges came around. Phyllis could tell that her friend was nervous, so she and Eve stayed with Carolyn for moral support.

"I don't really care about winning, of course," Carolyn said. "I know I've done a good job."

"Of course you have, dear," Eve said. "But a blue ribbon would be nice, wouldn't it? Or whatever they give out here."

"It certainly would. I'm fine without it, though."

Phyllis tried not to smile. Carolyn's competitive nature would never go away. At least, Phyllis hoped that it never would, because Carolyn wouldn't be Carolyn without it.

Quite a few spectators were milling around in the tent. Some of them followed the judges from place to place. Three men and two women would determine who moved on to the final round of competition the next day, and one of those men was Hiram Boudreau, Phyllis saw as the group of judges came up to the table.

"Howdy, ladies," Boudreau greeted them with a whiskery grin. "Now, you know I got to be impartial here, even though it's one of your friends who's the contestant, Evie."

"Of course, Hiram," Eve told him. "Carolyn wouldn't want it any other way, would you, dear?"

Carolyn was removing the lids from the containers. "Just taste what I've prepared," she said. "My food stands or falls on its own."

Boudreau leaned over the table and said, "What's that? Chili waffles? Let me get a taste of that!"

The judges all sampled the dishes. They had experience at this and were good at concealing any reactions they had, but Phyllis was watching them closely and her instincts told her that they liked everything they had tasted. Whether that would be enough to move Carolyn along in the contest, they would just have to wait and see.

Boudreau and the other judges moved on to the rest of the entries. Eventually, they had sampled everything and withdrew to an area near the bandstand to confer. There was still a lot of hubbub inside the tent, but it began to subside a little as the minutes ticked past. The contestants and their friends were eager to hear the results, and the longer they waited for that announcement, the more the tension grew.

Finally, Boudreau stepped up onto the platform with a wireless microphone in his hand and said, "Folks, gimme your attention. Normally, you put me up in front of this many people and I'm gonna do a little dancin', but I know y'all are anxious to find out who's movin' on in the contest and who ain't. Before I announce the results, I just want to say that there was some mighty fine eatin' in this tent today! The other judges and me, we had us the danged hardest time makin' up our minds that I ever recall in one o' these contests. But we got it figured out at last, and here are the contestants who are movin' on to the finals." He held up a piece of paper in his other hand. "I'll just call out the entry numbers, because right now that's all we know."

Phyllis looked at the pieces of paper taped to the table in front of Carolyn's entries. They had the number 99 printed on them, followed by the letters A, B, C, and D. She listened for that as Boudreau began reading the results from the sheet of paper.

Those results started with the number 7C, which brought cheers from the friends of that contestant and groans of disappointment from the ones lower than that who hadn't made the cut. A blend of similar reactions greeted each announcement from Boudreau. The numbers climbed rapidly, often skipping ten or twelve places at a time, and when Boudreau called out, "92A!", Phyllis's heart sank a little. Of course, logically that didn't mean Carolyn wouldn't advance, but Phyllis felt like it lessened the odds anyway.

She could tell that Carolyn was experiencing the same worry. She was breathing a little harder than usual, and her face was tense. Eve stood beside her, patting her on the shoulder, but Carolyn didn't seem to notice.

Then Boudreau shouted, "99D as in dog!" into the microphone. Carolyn released the big breath that evidently she'd been holding and closed her eyes for a moment in relief. Entry 99D was the chili waffles.

"I knew you could do it," Eve said.

"So did I," Phyllis added.

"Well, I couldn't have done anything if it hadn't been for Sam's chili," Carolyn said.

"It tasted so good it couldn't help but make my recipes better." She paused, then added, "And if you tell him I said that, I'll deny it!"

Phyllis laughed. It was good to forget about murder for a while.

Unfortunately, the case was still there, and as she listened to Hiram Boudreau calling out the rest of the entries that were going to advance, she tried once more to grasp whatever it was that had been nibbling at her brain for the past couple of days . . . only to have it slip away again.

CHAPTER 18

By the time Phyllis, Carolyn, and Eve got back to the trailer, Sam's chili was ready. He was stirring it occasionally and waiting for the judges to show up. There were too many contestants to have the judging for this preliminary round take place in the tent. The field would be narrowed down to the top thirty for the finals, and those contestants would move their grills into the tent and do their cooking there on Sunday.

When Sam saw the looks on the face of his three friends, he grinned and said, "I'd be willin' to bet that at least one of your dishes made the finals, Carolyn."

"The chili waffles," she said. "I think at least one of the others should have been picked, too, but I'll take what I can get. I'm still in the running, and that's what counts."

"Darn right," Sam agreed.

"The judges haven't been here yet?" Phyllis asked.

"Nope. They're still back up the line a ways, but they're workin' their way in this direction. Shouldn't be too much longer."

That prediction proved to be true. Thirty minutes later, Hiram Boudreau, Wendell Carson, and three other judges — all male this time — approached the War Wagon, trailed by a fairly large group of spectators that included McKayla. Phyllis looked around but didn't see Constable Chuck Snyder anywhere. Maybe he was deliberately keeping his distance from McKayla. That was a good idea. Also, he might be busy trying to get his hands on that forensics report. Phyllis hoped that was the case.

Sam had foam bowls ready for the judges. He ladled out five samples from each pot. With great deliberation, the judges tasted the chili. They were so solemn the whole thing reminded Phyllis of a wine tasting. She was a little surprised that the judges weren't talking about what sort of bouquet the chili had.

Each man also had a clipboard with papers on it for notes. They scribbled down their impressions, smiled and nodded to Sam, and moved on. Before he left, Hiram Boudreau gave Eve an exaggerated wink, which made her laugh.

"That man is incorrigible," Carolyn said.

"Thank goodness there are a few men in the world who still are," Eve said.

McKayla paused before following the rest of the spectators. She said to Phyllis, "Have you seen Constable Snyder today? I can't find him anywhere."

Phyllis didn't like to lie directly to anyone's face, so she said, "He was in town this morning. That's all I can tell you."

"You've got it all wrong about Chuck and me, you know," McKayla said, lowering her voice and glaring a little. "Everything would be fine if people would just leave us alone."

She walked off in an obvious huff, prompting Carolyn to ask, "What in the world was that all about?"

"Nothing important," Phyllis said. "She just thinks we're meddling in her love life."

Eve said, "Wait a minute. She asked about that young constable we were talking to this morning, Phyllis. Are you saying . . . ?"

"She's got a crush on him, that's all," Sam said. "And ol' Chuck seemed to takin' a little too much pleasure in it. That's all it amounted to."

"And the two of you knew about it." Eve nodded. "Now I understand why the constable was willing to help you. He's afraid of being accused of going after jailbait."

Phyllis shrugged. "I wouldn't try to ruin

his life unless he actually did something to deserve it, and as far as I know, he hasn't. He seemed genuinely embarrassed by the whole thing. But if he feels guilty enough to help solve a murder . . . well, I'm not going to stop him."

"That's a little cold-blooded," Carolyn commented.

"Nope," Sam said. "Hardboiled. That's us."

Phyllis changed the subject by asking, "How will the judges let you know if you made the finals?"

"They'll be around later," Sam said, "and then there'll be an official announcement in the tent tonight."

"So now we just have to wait?"

"Yep. But you know what they say about all good things comin' to those who wait."

Phyllis hoped that turned out to be true, although Sam's personality was such that he wouldn't be devastated if he failed to move on. He had been through a lot of adversity in his life, so not making the cut in a chili cook-off wouldn't bother him. He would just say that the whole experience had been fun and maybe decide to do it again next year.

Carolyn and Eve went inside the trailer. Sam had set up an awning to provide some shade outside, but the heat was still fierce, even underneath it. He leaned his head toward the door and told Phyllis, "You can go on in if you want. You don't have to stay out here and keep me company."

"I'm fine," she said. "I'd just as soon find out the results when you do. You've supported me in every contest I've entered. In everything I've done since I've known you, in fact."

"And I've had a mighty good time doin' it, too. I got to admit, wherever you are and whatever you're doin', you never let things get boring, Phyllis Newsom."

She laughed. "Is that a polite way of saying I'm a meddling old busybody who's always sticking my nose in other people's business? I've been accused of that, you know."

"You just try to find out the truth and make sure justice is done," Sam said. "If anybody complains about that, it's their problem, not yours."

Phyllis thought it was kind of Sam to say so. His attitude made it easier for her to deal with the doubts that sometimes crept into her mind about what she was doing.

Another hour went by before Phyllis looked along the row of motor homes and travel trailers and saw Wendell Carson walking toward them. She told Sam, "Here comes Mr. Carson. He was one of the judges, wasn't he?"

"Yep. He looks like he's got news, too. I just can't tell whether or not he's the bearer of glad tidin's."

As Carson walked up, though, a grin spread over his face, and Phyllis felt her spirits rise at that sight. Sam got to his feet and held out his hand.

"Congratulations, Mr. Fletcher," Carson said as he gripped Sam's hand. "Your Sam's Smokin' Red is going to be in the finals tomorrow."

"I'm mighty glad to hear it," Sam said. "It's an honor just to make the finals when this is my first time in the contest."

"Your chili was excellent. We had a lot of entries that deserved to move on. It's never easy, when you have so many to choose from."

Sort of like suspects in a murder, Phyllis thought.

Now that Sam had officially made the finals, he and Phyllis, along with Carolyn and Eve, celebrated with bowls of chili. Then Sam shut down the grill and took the pot inside to cool so that he could freeze the leftovers. Tomorrow he would start over inside the big tent, cooking his Sam's Smokin' Red.

With the competition part of the day behind them as darkness approached, Phyllis and the others changed clothes and strolled toward the tent, where many of the people in Cactus Bluff would congregate this evening for music and good fellowship. There were other, smaller parties going on around the encampment. Music of many different sorts filled the air.

As they walked along, they passed a trailer with a table set up outside where a card game was going on. Phyllis recognized one of the players as Jeff Porter. He glanced up, saw them going by, and called, "Hey, Fletcher, you play poker? You're welcome to sit in on the game if you want."

"No thanks," Sam replied with a shake of his head. "Gamblin' problem, you know."

"Oh, yeah, sure," Porter nodded.

As they walked on, Phyllis said to Sam, "You don't have a gambling problem."

"No, but that makes a good excuse for not playin', and fellas like Porter always understand and don't get offended."

"Because *he* has a gambling problem, you mean."

"Well, I don't know that," Sam said. "But he seems like the sort who might. He held that grudge over losin' to Hammersmith ever since last year, and here he is, playin' again. Maybe he just likes cards. Either way, I've never been much of a poker player."

"I played a few times and enjoyed it," Eve said. "Of course, the stakes were —"

"We don't care," Carolyn said. "Anyway, gambling is foolish."

"What about betting on cooking competitions?" Eve asked. "I'm sure quite a bit of *that* goes on."

"I never had anything to do with it. If people want to throw their money away, that's their business."

Sam said, "The one who's really gamblin' on this contest is Hiram Boudreau."

"How do you mean that?" Phyllis asked with a slight frown.

"Well, this weekend is the only time all year when any money to speak of flows into Cactus Bluff. The cook-off's got to make enough to support the town the rest of the year. I reckon that's why Boudreau didn't cancel the contest even after Hammersmith got himself blown up."

Eve said, "I don't think that's right. Hiram was in the oil business, you know. When he retired he had enough money to buy this entire town. It doesn't seem to me that he would depend on the cook-off to generate any real income."

That sounded logical to Phyllis, too. But then she remembered Boudreau saying that his effort to be a real estate developer hadn't worked out. There was one small mobile home park here in Cactus Bluff. What other projects had Boudreau tried to get started? Phyllis was far from an expert on such things, but she knew it was easy to pour a lot of money into real estate, only to be left with not much to show for it.

Maybe she ought to look into that when she had a chance, she told herself. Right now, however, from the corner of her eye she spotted Felicity, Josh, and Nick closing in on them.

"On your way to the party in the tent?" Felicity asked as the trio from *Inside Beat* came up to them.

"That's right," Phyllis said. "We have plenty to celebrate. Sam and Carolyn both made the finals."

"We heard," Josh said. "Congratulations."

"Thanks," Sam said.

"This isn't about a cooking contest anymore," Felicity said. "It's about murder now. Have you made any progress in the investigation, Phyllis?"

"I have a few ideas," Phyllis answered. "Nothing concrete yet."

"We're running out of time, you know.

The contest is over tomorrow. Some people will leave tomorrow evening, and the rest will be out of here first thing Monday morning. The suspects will be scattered all over the country."

Felicity was probably right about that, Phyllis knew. She said, "I don't know if the Rangers will allow everyone to leave —"

"They can't force that many people to stay here," Felicity interrupted. "They don't have any reasonable cause to lock down the whole town. All they'll do is get contact info from everybody. They've probably got the sheriff's department working on that already."

Phyllis hadn't really considered the time element. With the end of the cook-off serving as a deadline of sorts, the Rangers would feel even more pressure to make an arrest and close the case before that happened. Which meant that Sam was in even more danger of being taken into custody . . .

If the same thought had occurred to him, you couldn't tell it by looking at him, Phyllis thought as she glanced at him. He seemed as calm and unworried as always, confident in his innocence . . . and in her ability to prove that.

Felicity continued, "In the meantime, there's nothing for us to do except to keep on filing reports about the competition. How do you feel about making the finals on your first try, Mr. Fletcher?"

"Is this on camera?" Sam asked. A glance at Nick confirmed that it was. "Well, it's a real honor, of course. All these chili cooks are the real deal, let me tell you. I'm proud to be among 'em, and proud that my chili's been judged worthy to be in the finals."

"Are you going to win?" Felicity asked.

"Oh, shoot, I couldn't say about that. It's just a big honor to be part of the contest."

Felicity turned toward Nick and the camera. "Humble as always, that was Sam Fletcher, a finalist in the Great Chili Cook-Off. This is Felicity Prosper in Cactus Bluff, Texas." As Nick lowered the camera, Felicity sighed and went on, "Human interest stories!" Her disdain was obvious, but at least she'd been professional enough not to let it come through while Nick was recording.

"You should have interviewed Carolyn, too," Eve said. "She's in the finals of the leftover chili contest."

"Leftovers?" Felicity smirked and shook her head. "I don't think so." She gestured at Josh and Nick. "Come on, we'll get some shots of the musical performances." She looked over her shoulder at Phyllis as they walked away and added, "Solve that murder!

On camera, if you can."

As they started on toward the big tent, Carolyn said, "That young woman can be very annoying."

"She's . . . driven," Phyllis said.

"You're being kind to her."

A few minutes later, they joined the large crowd gathering in the tent as dusk settled down on the valley where Cactus Bluff was located. A musical group was already on the bandstand, half a dozen men in late middle age playing classic rock songs. The tables where the contest judging had taken place that afternoon — and would take place again the next day — had been moved back to create more room for dancing. Stands selling beer, soft drinks, bottled water, hot dogs, popcorn, and cotton candy had also been set up. There was a definite carnival atmosphere under the big striped tent top.

"Think I'll get a hot dog," Sam said. "You ladies want anything? My treat."

"I'd love a beer," Eve said.

"You got it."

"Do they have any of that frozen lemonade?" Carolyn asked. "It's too sweet, but after such a hot day I think it would be good."

"I'll bet they do," Sam said. "I'll check. Phyllis?"

She shook her head. "I'm fine right now, thanks."

"Be back in a minute." Sam's long legs carried him toward the area of the tent set aside for concessions.

The band started playing "Louie, Louie", belting out the unmistakable opening chords. Eve said, "I love this song!"

"The lyrics make absolutely no sense," Carolyn said.

"They do under the right circumstances. You just had to be there, dear." Eve drifted toward the bandstand. Carolyn went with her.

Phyllis was still standing there, smiling after her friends, when someone came up and touched her on the arm. She jumped a little, even though she tried not to.

"It's all right, Mrs. Newsom," Constable Chuck Snyder said as she turned to him. "I've got something for you."

He held out a file folder. Phyllis could tell he was trying to be discreet about it. She took it and said, "Is this . . . ?"

"Yeah. You told me to try to get a look at it, but I was able to get a copy."

She opened the folder, and in the light from the lanterns set up around the inside of the tent, she saw the reports from the forensics team and the county fire marshal on the explosion that had killed Joe D. Hammersmith. Quickly, she scanned the typed words and looked at the photographs and diagrams that accompanied them.

Phyllis was still trying to digest everything when a hand suddenly reached in from the side, flipped the folder closed, and then took it away from her. Her startled gaze rose to the rugged face of Sergeant Martin Culbertson as he said, "I'll take that . . . and I'm listening for a good reason why I shouldn't arrest the both of you."

CHAPTER 19

Chuck looked like he was ready to panic, but Phyllis met Culbertson's accusing stare squarely. She said, "There's a very good reason. You're going to arrest my friend Sam, and he didn't cause that explosion."

"You sound mighty sure about that."

"Wouldn't you be sure, Sergeant, if you were talking about *your* best friend?"

Culbertson narrowed his eyes at her and said, "I might feel that way, but I wouldn't let my feelings stand in the way of evidence. And the only physical evidence we've got in this case —"

"Points to Sam, I know. You can put him on the scene. But a thousand other people walked past that grill and motor home. *They* were on the scene, too."

"We can't prove that any of them touched the grill," Culbertson pointed out.

"The grill's not what caused the explosion," Phyllis said.

Culbertson narrowed his eyes at her and asked, "What makes you say that?"

Phyllis pointed at the folder in the Ranger's hand. "The investigation by the fire marshal, as well as the other forensics evidence, indicates that the ignition point of the fire was in the vicinity of the grill, but the cylinder itself wasn't breached prior to the blast. The cause of the explosion was propane that leaked out of the ASME tank built into the motor home, collected underneath the vehicle, and seeped out near the grill. When Hammersmith went to light one of the burners on the grill, it ignited that collected propane, which then set off the cylinder inside the grill as well as the gas tank on the motor home."

The words spilled out of her mouth without her really knowing what she was going to say ahead of time, but even as she spoke, the things she had learned, as well as the speculation she had done, all seemed to link together, one bit of information after the other, to form a coherent chain of events. If she had spent a lot of time mulling it all over, she might not have been able to discern the pattern as clearly, but the threat represented by the angry Texas Ranger sergeant had forced her brain into overdrive.

Culbertson and Chuck both stared at her.

Culbertson found his voice first and said, "You got all that from a few glances at a report?"

"You said it yourself, Sergeant. I have some experience in murder cases."

Culbertson tapped the folder against the palm of his other hand. "It just so happens that a theory pretty close to yours has been stirring around in my head. I had to study this report for a couple of hours first, though. You really do have a knack for this sort of thing." He looked from Phyllis to Chuck and back again. "But that doesn't change the fact that you two interfered in an active investigation."

"An investigation that Constable Snyder should have been part of to start with," Phyllis said. "He knows this area and the people who live around here."

"Thanks, Mrs. Newsom," Chuck said.

Culbertson shook his head, though, and said, "That doesn't matter. Hammersmith only came to Cactus Bluff once a year, for this blasted chili cook-off, and he didn't really have anything to do with any of the locals. My partner and I have questioned enough of them to know that. The only people he interacted with were the other folks who came for the contest. The murderer has to be one of them. So the constable's background isn't going to be any help to us."

"Sam never even met Hammersmith until less than twelve hours before he was killed," Phyllis said, unable to keep the frustration she felt out of her voice. "What possible motive could he have had? Just to eliminate the defending champion in the competition? Are you really going to try to sell that to a district attorney to get a murder charge, Sergeant, let alone to a jury for a conviction?"

Culbertson's jaw tightened. Phyllis knew she had put her finger on the weak spot in the case the Ranger was trying to build. Someone with a history of trouble with Hammersmith might have gone to the trouble to blow him up like that, but a man who had just met him and had nothing against him?

"What's goin' on here?" The question came from behind Phyllis and made her look around. Sam stood there with a hot dog — covered with chili, relish, and cheese — in one hand and a soft drink cup in the other.

Culbertson nodded to him and said, "Evening, Mr. Fletcher. I was just saying hello to Mrs. Newsom and Constable Snyder."

"I sort of expected to see more of you around, Sergeant," Sam said. "You must've been busy today."

"Busy enough."

"Still looking into that explosion?"

"We are," Culbertson said.

"I'll wish you luck, then. Hope you find the killer before the contest is over."

"We will, Mr. Fletcher." Culbertson's head moved in a curt nod. "You can count on that." He smiled thinly at Phyllis. "Enjoy your evening, Mrs. Newsom."

The Ranger turned and walked away, weaving through the crowd in the tent and disappearing from sight. He took the file folder with him, of course, which brought a sigh from Phyllis. She would have liked to study its contents more closely. She would just have to be satisfied, she told herself, with enough of a look to be able to put together a theory that even Sergeant Culbertson thought was plausible. As soon as she got a chance, she would discuss it with Sam as well.

"I got a feelin' there was more goin' on here than a friendly chat," Sam commented once Culbertson was gone.

"It wasn't friendly," Chuck confirmed. "I don't think the sergeant likes any of us very much right now."

Sam looked at Phyllis and said, "What did you do?"

"Constable Snyder got his hands on the report from the fire marshal and the sheriff's department forensics team, and we were just taking a look at it when Sergeant Culbertson showed up." Something occurred to Phyllis. "How did he know you had it?"

"One of the deputies I sounded out about it must have sold me out," Chuck said. "That'll teach me to trust people, even if they are old rodeo pals."

Sam said, "I'm surprised the sergeant didn't arrest the two of you."

"He threatened to," Phyllis said. "But I think I gave him too much to think about."

"He made a good point," Chuck said. "Nobody around here would have had any reason to kill Hammersmith. The murderer has to be someone from out of town."

Phyllis nodded slowly, unable to escape the logic of that idea.

Sam took a bite of the hot dog, chewed, and swallowed. "I hate to say it, but the chili on this dog is dang near as good as mine. Not quite, mind you, but in the same neighborhood."

"Did you take Carolyn and Eve their drinks?" Phyllis asked.

"Yep, dropped 'em off before I came back

over here." Sam grinned. "Carolyn even seemed to be enjoyin' herself a little, listenin' to the music. Even if it is rock an' roll."

"I guess I'd better circulate around and make sure everything stays peaceful," Chuck said. "I'm still the constable around here . . . at least for now."

Sam watched the young man walk off, then said, "What do you reckon he means by that?"

"Well, now he's in trouble with the Rangers, and he already has an underage girl pursuing him," Phyllis said. "I suppose he's worried that one or both of those problems will catch up to him and cost him his job."

"I hope that doesn't happen. He seems like a nice enough young fella. A little out of his depth, maybe."

"It probably didn't help matters that I forced him to help me. I feel a little guilty about that." Phyllis thought about what she had learned. "Only a little, though." She looked around. "Let's find a quieter spot."

They walked to one of the rear corners of the tent and went behind one of the tables. A few folding metal chairs were still sitting around, so Phyllis pulled over a couple of them and they sat down. Sam continued eating his hot dog while Phyllis said, "I was right about how it wasn't the propane cylinder in Hammersmith's grill that exploded first, even though the area around the grill was where the fire started."

"It was a fire first, not an explosion?"

"That's what the evidence indicates. But it all went so fast after ignition that anyone would think it was all one blast. My idea is that someone sabotaged the propane tank on Hammersmith's motor home so that the gas leaked out and collected under the vehicle. There was enough of it to reach the grill."

"So when Hammersmith went to light it . . . *blooie!*"

"Yes, blooie . . . if you want to get technical about it." Phyllis smiled.

Sam nodded and said, "Could've happened that way. There's a valve on those tanks that lets you bleed off the propane. It's there next to the fill valve, and sometimes people have covers on those that you can lock up, to keep people from messin' with 'em. You could still make the propane leak out by breachin' the tubing, though. Wouldn't take much. And since it's underneath the motor home, people would be less likely to see what you were doin'."

"From what I saw of that report, I'm convinced that's what happened."

"But it doesn't make any difference," Sam said. "Whether the killer sabotaged the cylinder in the grill or the tank on the motor home, you're left with the fact that it had to be somebody who knew what he was doin' *and* had a grudge against Hammersmith." Sam waved a hand to indicate the crowd. "You've still got the same pool of suspects you always had."

"I know," Phyllis said, trying not to feel discouraged.

The rock and roll cover band finished their set. Before another group of musicians could take the stage, Hiram Boudreau appeared on the platform, bony arms extended over his head as he clapped his hands.

"Let's give 'em a big round of applause, folks!" he called. "That was some mighty fine music. We got more comin' up. In fact, anybody who wants to come up here and jam is welcome. But before we move on to that, I want to announce the names of all the contestants who'll be in the finals of all the contests tomorrow, so listen up!"

Sam finished his hot dog and threw the little paper boat it came in into a plastic garbage can. Phyllis said, "Let's move up to the front so we can hear better."

"We already know that both Carolyn and I are in the finals," Sam said.

Phyllis smiled. "Yes, but I'd like to hear it again. I'm proud of my friends."

"I'm not gonna argue with that," Sam said with a grin of his own.

They worked their way forward through the crowd until they were near the bandstand. Phyllis heard Eve say, "There they are!" A moment later, she and Carolyn slid through a narrow gap in the press of people to join Phyllis and Sam.

Less than a minute later, Boudreau announced Carolyn's name as one of the finalists in the leftover chili competition. Phyllis could tell that her friend was pleased and proud of the recognition, and she was happy for Carolyn. She had no idea if the chili waffles stood a chance of winning, but if that happened, it would be a nice touch for the article she was writing for *A Taste of Texas*.

Boudreau worked his way through the rest of the list, including Sam, who just nodded confidently as Phyllis, Eve, and Carolyn applauded at the mention of his name.

Phyllis heard some other familiar names, too. Kurt Middleton, Royce Glennister, and Jeff Porter had all reached the finals. Maybe with Joe D. Hammersmith dead, one of them would actually win this time . . . although that still seemed awfully far-fetched to Phyllis as a motive for murder.

Of course, each of those men — and there was no telling how many more — had other reasons to hold a grudge against Hammersmith as well.

Boudreau made several other announcements, including reading off the license numbers of cars where the drivers had left the lights on, and then said, "All you chili cooks who are in the finals will need to be set up here in the tent by ten o'clock in the mornin', ready to cook. Y'all know the rules. There'll be cook-off officials checkin' your grills and ingredients to make sure everything is the way it's supposed to be, and may the best chili cooker win!

"That's for tomorrow, though," he went on. "Tonight we're here to have a good time, which means more music! Who's comin' up here to entertain us next?"

B.J. Sawyer and the Lavaca River Boys took the stage and immediately launched into "Foggy Mountain Breakdown", the sprightly bluegrass standard they had been playing when Phyllis and the others first heard them two nights earlier. Evidently the song was one of Hiram Boudreau's favorites, too, because he started dancing back and forth across the bandstand in the same sort of wild abandon he had displayed on the previous occasion. His scrawny arms flapped, and his knobby, scraped knees pumped high. Sam laughed, clapped his hands in time to the music, and said, "I think he's tryin' to do a chicken dance, but it's not like any chicken I've ever seen."

"Unless it was one with its head cut off," Carolyn added as she smiled and clapped, too.

Phyllis nodded her head to the rhythm, and as if the music had an effect on her thoughts, they began to dance around, too. She lifted her hands, about to clap along with Sam, Carolyn, and Eve, but then stopped short and stood there with her hands raised in front of her. A moment passed, and then two. Then she gave a little shake of her head and lowered her hands.

More than once, one of her friends had seen the same sort of look on her face that she wore now and asked her if she had just solved the case. Tonight, though, none of them were looking at her. They were all watching the stage, enjoying the music and Hiram Boudreau's antics.

But whether they were aware of it or not, Phyllis now had a pretty good idea who had killed Joe D. Hammersmith.

What she didn't know was *why*.

CHAPTER 20

Phyllis managed to hide her distraction during the rest of the evening. She never liked to discuss her theories until she was certain of them, although sometimes she would share some of her thoughts with Sam.

In this case, however, the idea she had was so nebulous, and supported by only one real piece of evidence, that she wanted to keep it to herself until she had a chance to find out more. She told herself that under the circumstances, she might as well just relax and enjoy the music and the festivities . . .

But that wasn't easy, knowing that a murderer was on the loose in Cactus Bluff.

Still, she was confident that none of her friends knew what was really going on in her brain as she walked back to the War Wagon with Sam, Carolyn, and Eve later that evening. When they reached the trailer, Carolyn and Eve went on inside, but Sam gestured toward the lawn chairs and asked,

"Would you like to sit out here for a while before you turn in?"

"Actually, I believe I would," Phyllis said. The air had cooled off quickly once the sun was down, as it had a tendency to do in this region, and there was a pleasant breeze blowing over the encampment. Phyllis and Sam sat down side by side. She closed her eyes for a moment and sighed, not . . . content . . . exactly, since the murder case was still hanging over their heads, but she was glad to be here with Sam.

"Are you looking forward to tomorrow?" she asked.

"Well, sure," he said. "It'll be a big day. I'm not worried so much about who wins. I just like knowin' that more folks will get to try my chili. It's fun, you know."

"I know. That's one of the best parts about being in these competitions. You want people to enjoy what you're doing."

"Yep. I figure just bein' part of it is winnin' enough. Anything else is gravy." Sam paused. "Hmm . . . chili gravy." A grin lit up his face. "Chili SOS!"

"Next year," Phyllis said with a smile of her own.

They sat there for another half-hour, not talking much, just enjoying the night air and each other's company. Phyllis had too much going on in her brain to relax completely, though, and she found herself anxious to spend some time on her computer.

"I believe I'll go on in," she told Sam as she got to her feet.

"I might sit out here for a while longer, if you don't mind."

"Not at all," she said as she bent over and kissed him on the forehead. "Good night."

" 'Night."

She went in, sat down on the loveseat, and picked up the laptop from the little table in front of it. A quick check of her email didn't turn up anything that had to be dealt with at the moment, so she was able to begin searching.

She started with county tax records and moved on to satellite images. From there she began digging deeper into on-line newspaper archives.

As often happened at times like these, Phyllis got lost in what she was doing, so she wasn't aware of how much time had passed until Carolyn said, "Good grief, Phyllis, what are you doing? It's the middle of the night. Can't you sleep? Wait a minute. You don't look like you've even been to bed."

"I haven't," Phyllis said as she looked up from the computer to see her pajama-clad friend standing in front of the refrigerator.

"I got up to get something to drink, then realized the light was still on in here," Carolyn said. "You were staring at that computer like your mind was a million miles away —" Carolyn stopped short and drew in a breath. "You've figured it out, haven't you?"

"Not all of it," Phyllis answered honestly. "I still don't know what's at the very bottom of things, although I can make a guess."

"You need to tell that Texas Ranger, first thing in the morning."

Phyllis thought about the promise she had made to Chuck Snyder and said, "We'll see." Felicity was expecting to be let in on the scoop, as well. Phyllis wasn't sure she wanted to share what she had figured out with either of them just yet, not until she was sure she was right.

"But there's nothing I can do about it tonight," she said as she closed the laptop. "Nothing except get some rest. Tomorrow will be a big day."

Carolyn looked at her and said, "I have a hunch you're not just talking about the finals of the Great Chili Cook-Off."

By morning, after a few hours of sleep, the theory Phyllis had put together the night before had crystalized in her brain. As she examined it in the light of a new day, she was more convinced than ever that she was right. She had to have proof, though, and to get that she would need help.

Sam was already outside the War Wagon with his pickup, getting ready to move his grill to the big tent for the finals. Phyllis pitched in to help him. She didn't say anything about what she had been thinking. If she shared her theory with him, it would distract him from the contest, and she didn't see any reason to do that.

They had everything loaded up and Sam was about ready to leave for the tent when Sergeant Martin Culbertson walked up. "Good morning," he said, nodding to both Phyllis and Sam.

"I reckon whether it is or not is sort of up to you, Sergeant," Sam said dryly.

"I thought I'd stop by and wish you luck in the finals today," Culbertson said. "Also, I'd like to have a word with you when the contest is over, so I'd appreciate it if you stay around where I can find you."

"Don't leave town, is that what you're sayin'?"

"I'd appreciate it."

"Sure," Sam said. "I'm not goin' anywhere. The contest will take most of the day, and after that I won't be in any hurry to go anywhere. We're not headin' back to Weatherford until tomorrow."

Culbertson nodded and said, "Just so we understand each other."

"We do," Sam assured him.

Culbertson touched a finger to his hat brim and said, "Mrs. Newsom," then turned to walk off.

Sam glanced at Phyllis and said, "You look like you're so mad you're about ready to chew nails."

"He's going to arrest you for Hammersmith's murder," Phyllis said. Her voice shook a little from the depth of the emotion she felt. She couldn't help it. "That's what he was telling you."

"I know," Sam said calmly. "I think he feels a mite bad about it, though. That's why he didn't go ahead and clap the cuffs on me right now. He's gonna let me finish out the competition because he doesn't really want to arrest me. I'm the only suspect he has any actual evidence against, though."

"And it's purely circumstantial! He knows he can't make a case, but he's going to put you through that anyway. It's not right."

"Well, who knows . . . Maybe he'll find the real killer before the day is over."

Phyllis came close to telling Sam right then and there about what she had figured

253

out, but in the end she kept it to herself. When he climbed into the pickup, she told him, "I'll be over at the tent later with Carolyn and Eve. As soon as Carolyn's contest is over this morning, we'll be your cheering section."

He grinned at her. "Eve's probably waved a few pom-poms in her time, but I don't know about Carolyn."

Despite everything, Phyllis had to laugh at that image. She lifted a hand in a wave as Sam drove off.

Then she got to work.

She told Carolyn and Eve that she would be back later and then walked toward Cactus Bluff's business block. If anything, the town was even more crowded this morning. Phyllis supposed some chili aficionados came in just for the final day of the competition. She noticed more news media trucks, as well. This was the high point of the year for the semi-ghost town.

Phyllis had just reached the sidewalk when someone behind her called, "Mrs. Newsom! Phyllis!" She knew the voice instantly and wasn't surprised when she turned and saw Felicity, Josh, and Nick coming toward her.

"Good morning —" Phyllis began.

"Don't think you can get away from us," Felicity said. "This is the last day of the contest. This murder gets solved today, and we're sticking with you until it is!"

Phyllis managed not to groan, but she had to make an effort. Having the trio from *Inside Beat* around was going to make things more difficult. On the walk over here, she had decided that she would have to take Chuck Snyder into her confidence because she needed his help, but Felicity and her two faithful followers would just complicate things.

"I'm just taking a walk," she told them. Actually, she'd been looking for Chuck, but she hadn't spotted his Jeep yet. "And then I'll be going over to the tent to spend the day with Sam while the competition is going on. I'm afraid I'm not going to be doing anything newsworthy."

"I don't believe that for a second," Felicity snapped. "Look, we helped you solve that other case, didn't we? Let us give you a hand with this one."

Phyllis thought about it for a moment and then nodded. "Actually, there *is* something you can do," she said.

Felicity leaned forward with an eager look on her beautiful face. "What is it?"

"All the chili cooks who are in the finals will be setting up in the tent this morning. You probably need to interview them anyway. While you're doing that, check to see if any of them are using a Lydecker 6500 grill."

Felicity's carefully arched eyebrows rose as her eyes widened. "Is that important?"

"It could be very important," Phyllis said, dropping her voice to a conspiratorial tone as she went on, "It's the same type of grill that Joe D. Hammersmith used."

"OMG," Felicity breathed. "Of course! We can check that out, can't we, guys?"

"A Lydecker 6500," Josh said. "Got it!" He turned to Nick. "Can you remember that, too, and get a shot of it if we find one?"

"I can get a shot of anything," Nick said.

Felicity asked, "Will that be the murderer? The man who's using a grill like that?"

"I don't know yet," Phyllis said, "but it's important, I can tell you that much."

Felicity nodded and said, "All right, now we're getting somewhere. Come on."

They were getting somewhere, all right, Phyllis thought as she watched the trio head for the big tent. They were getting out of her hair — and out of possible danger — which was all she'd been trying to accomplish by sending them on this wild goose chase. She had no idea how many Lydecker 6500s they would find — or if they would find any.

But now she was free to continue her search for Constable Chuck Snyder.

Before she could do that, Hiram Boudreau came out the front door of the Boudreau Hotel and stopped to greet her with a big grin.

"Good mornin' to you, Miz Newsom," he said. "Where's that feisty little friend o' yours?"

"You mean Eve, of course."

"A good name for the lady. Of course, I'm Hiram, not Adam, and Cactus Bluff's not exactly the Garden of Eden —"

"Eve's back at the trailer with Carolyn," Phyllis said, not particularly wanting to know where Boudreau was going with that line of thought. "Either that or they've already headed over to the big tent for this morning's competition."

"Well, then, I'll go find 'em and wish Miz Wilbarger the best of luck. I'm not judgin' this morning, so I don't have to be quite so impartial anymore. Of course, as the Grand High Poobah of Cactus Bluff, I still can't play favorites, even though I might want to."

"I'm sure Carolyn would rather win or lose fair and square," Phyllis said. "She's competitive, but she always wants the contests she enters to be fair."

"That's the way to be, all right." Boudreau lifted a hand in farewell and moved off along the sidewalk with a little natural boogie in his stride. Phyllis watched him go and then shook her head.

As she turned away, she saw the constable's Jeep roll to a stop along the sidewalk nearby, parking in an unloading zone in front of the hotel. Chuck climbed out, nodded to Phyllis, and asked, "Have you seen that Ranger this morning?"

"As a matter of fact, I have. He came by the trailer earlier to tell Sam not to leave town after the finals this afternoon."

"Uh-oh," Chuck said. "That doesn't sound good."

"I know. I think there's so much pressure on him to make an arrest that he's going to take Sam into custody, even though it's obvious that he's no killer."

"Obvious to us, maybe. Juries really put a high degree of trust in forensic evidence these days, though. You'd hate to think that an innocent man could be convicted on the basis of a fingerprint, but stranger things have happened."

Phyllis knew that was true, and it was one reason she didn't want Sam to be arrested. She had faith in the legal system, but at the same time she knew it could take some wildly divergent paths at times and result in miscarriages of justice.

"I'm working on making sure that doesn't happen," she said, "but I have a question for you, Constable."

"You might as well call me Chuck," he said. "We're sort of in this mess together."

"Two questions, actually: do you keep a record of all the traffic citations you write? And where is Hiram Boudreau's house?"

"The mayor doesn't have a house," Chuck said, answering the second question first. "He lives here in the hotel, on the top floor. It's all one suite up there." Chuck pointed upward to indicate the hotel's top level, then rubbed his chin. "And sure, I keep copies of all the citations. They're in a file cabinet in my office, over in the town hall."

"Have you ever written a ticket for Joe D. Hammersmith? A speeding ticket, maybe?"

Chuck frowned and shook his head. "Not that I recall. I told you, nobody speeds in Cactus Bluff during the weekend of the chili cook-off."

"This probably would have been some other time of year, not during the cook-off."

"No, I'm still drawing a blank. Sorry. Is it important?"

"It *could* be," Phyllis said, trying not to show the disappointment she felt. This wasn't a vital part of the theory she had built, but it *was* involved, and she was afraid that if one element collapsed, it would lead to more and more breakdowns until the idea proved to be worthless. "Is there a chance someone else might have written a ticket like that?"

"Well, sure. Ken Bristol might have."

"Ken?" Phyllis said. "The man who works for the security company?"

"Sure. He works part-time as a deputy constable, too." Chuck smiled. "I can't be on duty around the clock."

"No, of course not. Is he your only deputy?"

"Yeah, between us we handle the job. And he can write traffic tickets just like I can. I can go over to the office and check the files if it would help."

"It could help a lot," Phyllis said.

"All right. Where can I find you?"

"I'll be at the tent in a little while."

Chuck nodded. "I'll find you there."

He left the Jeep where it was and walked across the street. Phyllis looked around, then took a deep breath and went into the hotel.

CHAPTER 21

Even though most people who came to Cactus Bluff for the Great Chili Cook-Off brought their travel trailers or motor homes, this was still the one weekend of the year when it was impossible to get a room at the Boudreau Hotel. Phyllis had read on the competition's website that reservations needed to be made at least a year in advance, and even that usually involved just getting on a waiting list.

Because of that, the lobby was crowded, and for once Phyllis didn't mind getting into a mob of people. That made it less likely anyone would notice her.

The Boudreau Hotel had started its existence as the Cactus House back in the late Nineteenth Century, when the mines were booming and so was the town. It was a four-story brick structure that took up half a block, with balconies attached to the upper three floors. Over the decades it had fallen somewhat into disrepair, but after Hiram Boudreau had bought it, he'd had the place remodeled, repaired, and refurbished. According to the website, it still had all of its Old West charm. The lobby featured marble floors, a lot of polished wood and brass, old-fashioned ceiling fans and chandeliers, and an assortment of potted palms, cacti, and other plants. On one side of the lobby was the arched entrance to the Gold Nugget Bar. Even at this early hour, the bar appeared to be doing quite a bit of business.

Phyllis wasn't interested in drinking. She walked past the bar to a curving staircase with a gilt balustrade. People were going up and down the stairs, laughing and talking, so she joined the stream of jocular humanity and headed up.

With each flight of stairs, the steps grew less crowded. By the time Phyllis started up from the third floor landing toward the fourth floor, she was the only one on the stairs, which made sense if Hiram Boudreau was the only occupant on the hotel's top level.

There was a short hallway at the top of the stairs, situated so that most of the space on this floor was to Phyllis's left. There were doors on both side of the hall, but when she tried the one on the right, she found it unlocked and quickly saw that it led into a small storage room. She closed that door and turned to the one on the left.

It was locked, which came as no surprise. Hiram Boudreau might own Cactus Bluff, but that didn't mean he would be comfortable going off and leaving his living quarters wide open. Phyllis fiddled with the knob for a few minutes but couldn't get it open. She had never learned how to pick a lock. She'd told Sam that just because they worked sometimes for Jimmy D'Angelo, that didn't make them private eyes, and her inability to break into Boudreau's suite was proof of that.

The window at the front end of the hallway looked out on the balcony, though. Phyllis went to it, saw that it was the kind with old-fashioned thumb locks, and twisted them open. It took her only a moment to lift the pane, and since she was wearing jeans she had no trouble stepping over the sill onto the balcony.

From up here, she could see the broad sweep of the valley in the morning light. She felt a little like a character in one of those Western novels Sam read. A cattle baroness, maybe, surveying her ranch.

That flight of fancy lasted only a second. She had more important things to think about. Aware that people could see her up here if they happened to lift their eyes that far, she moved hurriedly along the balcony toward several more windows that opened onto it. These windows had to be in Boudreau's suite, and Phyllis could only hope that one of them would be unlocked.

The first one wasn't. She made a face and went to the next one, found that she couldn't get in there, either. That left just one window. If it wouldn't open, she would have to abandon this idea and hope that whatever evidence Chuck might turn up would be enough to convince Sergeant Culbertson of the truth — or at least to keep the investigation going and not arrest Sam.

Phyllis reached down and grasped the bottom of the last window. It resisted her efforts to lift it. She stepped back and heaved a frustrated sigh.

"Why, Mrs. Newsom, what're you doin' up here? If I didn't know better, I'd say you were tryin' to break into my suite."

Phyllis took a quick step back from the window and half-turned toward the far end of the balcony where she had emerged from the fourth floor hall. Hiram Boudreau stood there, a puzzled look on his whiskery face, dressed as he had been when she encountered him down on the sidewalk a short time earlier, in combat boots, cut-off jeans, t-shirt, and straw hat.

"Mr. Boudreau, you startled me," Phylis said as she tried to still her racing heartbeat.

"Sorry. Didn't mean to do that. I just got curious when I looked back and saw you talkin' to the constable, then you went into the hotel." Boudreau grinned as he came a step closer. "Actually, I've never minded classy ladies tryin' to sneak into my room. I just figured it'd be a lot more likely it was your friend Evie I found up here."

"That's not it at all." Phyllis saw movement behind Boudreau, felt her heart jump again in alarm, and then relief surged through her as Constable Chuck Snyder stepped through the open window onto the balcony. She took a breath and said, "I was trying to get in so I could look for more evidence to prove you murdered Joe D. Hammersmith, Mr. Boudreau."

Boudreau's jaw sagged as he stared at Phyllis. She saw hate and anger flash in his eyes, though, and that reaction confirmed the educated guesses she had made. He controlled it, but not quickly enough to keep her from noticing.

"I think the heat's been too much for you, ma'am. You're not thinkin' straight. Ol' Joe D. and I were good friends. There's no way I'd ever hurt him. Besides, he was the defendin' champion of the cook-off. His dyin' was bad for business."

Phyllis nodded and said, "That's why I knew you had to be really desperate to do such a thing as sabotaging the propane tank on the bottom of his motor home. Hammersmith had to represent a bigger threat to you than any damage his death might do to the cook-off. You need the money from this competition to keep going, because you're just about broke, aren't you?"

Phyllis was trying very hard not to look at Chuck, who had frozen about ten feet behind Boudreau with his hand on the stun gun holstered at his waist. Chuck was breathing shallowly and not making a sound. So far, it seemed that Boudreau wasn't aware of his presence.

"How in blazes do you figure I'm broke?" Boudreau asked. "I told you, I sold my oil company —"

"A/B Explorations, I know," Phyllis said. "I also know that your partner Harlan Anders didn't want to sell and that he died while undergoing treatment for cancer. He would have passed away soon anyway, but the corporation that put in an offer for your company was threatening to withdraw it. Anders didn't want to sell, so you helped him along somehow."

"You're sayin' that I murdered my old partner Harlan?" Boudreau laughed. "That's crazy!"

"Is it? Then why did you give his children eighty per cent of the money from the sale? I think it was because they were suspicious, and you paid them off to keep them from looking too closely at their father's death. You still got a nice chunk of money . . . or you would have if you hadn't been sued by the corporation that bought A/B Exploration for fraud because you falsified the company's records and overvalued it. You had to settle with them, and that took most of what you had left. You thought you'd recoup those losses by buying this town and developing it as a resort and retirement community, but that didn't work out, either. I've seen the property tax records, as well as the roads and other work you had put in on housing developments that never panned out because you ran out of money. Then you got the idea of staging this chili cook-off and that's kept you afloat, but you're not doing well enough to pay blackmail to Joe D. Hammersmith from now on. Did he find out you were responsible for Anders' death? Maybe promised to help Anders' children bleed you for what little you have left?"

"You . . . you don't know what you're talkin' about," Boudreau sputtered. "This is all just some crazy notion you dreamed up. There's not one thing in the world to back up what you've been sayin'!"

"What about that?" Phyllis asked, pointing.

Boudreau looked down. "My knees? What about 'em?"

"You scraped them crawling under Hammersmith's motor home on Thursday night. I saw you dancing to the Lavaca River Boys' music at their motor home on Thursday night, remember? Your knees were fine then. A little on the knobby side, but unmarked. The next day, they were red and raw. They've scabbed up some since then, but you can still tell what happened to them."

"Scraped knees?" Boudreau said, trying to sound astounded. "You think scraped knees makes a man guilty of murder?"

"That's just what got me wondering what you'd done to them," Phyllis said. "Nobody ever considered you a suspect, Mr. Boudreau, but once I started thinking about it and seeing what else I could find, I was able to put together a theory."

Boudreau snorted. "A theory," he repeated. "That's all it is. You don't have any proof."

"I'll bet the Rangers can come up with some," Phyllis said, "once I've talked to Sergeant Culbertson and convinced him to take a nice, long look at your financial history . . . and Hammersmith's. The things you've done will have left a paper trail. There might even be withdrawals from your account that match deposits in his."

"Maybe back in March," Chuck said, finally speaking up and causing Boudreau to give a startled jump. As Boudreau turned to look at the constable, Chuck held up a piece of paper and went on, "That's when Ken gave Hammersmith a speeding ticket."

Phyllis nodded. "That proves Hammersmith was here other times besides the chili cook-off."

"You . . . you're tryin' to frame me," Boudreau stammered. "None o' this is true —"

"Then you don't have anything to worry about when Mrs. Newsom and I talk to the Rangers. But for now, Mayor, you'd better come with me —"

A snarl twisted Boudreau's face. "That's right, I'm the mayor!" he said. "Cactus Bluff is *my* town, damn it! Nobody's gonna take it away from me, it or anything else I've ever worked for! Harlan and I had a chance to clean up, and he wasn't gonna ruin it for me —"

He stopped short, perhaps realizing that he was about to say too much . . . or that he already had.

"We'll go over to the office," Chuck said, taking a step toward Boudreau and lifting his hand. "We can wait there while I call Ken and have him find the Rangers —"

"Mrs. Newsom! Hey! Phyllis!"

At the sound of that insistent shouting, Phyllis and Chuck both turned their heads to look across the street. Felicity Prosper stood there, along with Josh and Nick. Felicity went on, "We found a Lydecker 6500 —"

Boudreau lunged at Chuck. Phyllis saw sunlight reflect on metal as Chuck let out a pained yelp. He stumbled back a couple of steps and pressed his hand to his side as blood welled between his fingers.

"Get outta my way, damn it!" Boudreau cried. He turned as Phyllis took an instinctive step toward him and slashed at her with the knife he had taken from a pocket of his cut-off jeans. She jerked back. "Nobody's gonna take my town away from me!"

Chuck was fumbling with his other hand at the stun gun, but he wasn't able to get it free of the holster as Boudreau came at him

270

again with the bloody knife. Before Boudreau could stab the constable again, long, tanned legs flashed as McKayla Carson leaped through the open window. She thrust out both arms and rammed her hands against Boudreau's chest as she shouted, "Leave him alone!"

Boudreau didn't weigh a great deal. The shove made him reel backward toward the railing at the edge of the balcony. McKayla charged after him and hit him again. The railing cracked under the impact, and with a terrified wail, Boudreau fell through it and plummeted toward the street below.

Phyllis had caught up to McKayla by now and grabbed her to keep her from falling, too. She pulled the girl back from the broken railing. McKayla seemed to recover her senses after the attack and rushed to Chuck's side. The constable had sagged to the floor of the balcony and was sitting there with his face pale and drawn.

"Chuck! Darling!"

"It's not that bad," Chuck said in a strained voice. "It's just a deep cut in my side. I've taken first aid classes. I'll be all right —"

He swayed and passed out, falling over on his side.

Phyllis looked over the balcony railing. An

even bigger crowd had gathered and sur-
rounded Hiram Boudreau, who lay on the
pavement moaning. From the looks of it,
one or both of his legs were broken, but he
didn't appear to have any other serious
injuries. He must have landed on some of
the pedestrians clogging the street, Phyllis
thought, and they had broken his fall.

"Phyllis! Hey, Phyllis!"

She looked up and saw Felicity on the far
sidewalk, giving her two thumbs-up. Beside
her, Nick was recording, and Josh just
looked a little stunned. Phyllis knew what
the lead story on the next edition of *Inside
Beat* was going to be.

America's Crime-Busting Grandma had
struck again, and this time Felicity had it all
on tape . . . or whatever they used these
days.

CHAPTER 22

Sam held up the yellow ribbon and said, "With all the excitement goin' on around here today, third place doesn't seem like such a big deal."

"Don't be ridiculous," Phyllis told him. "Winning third place in a major chili cook-off on your first try is a huge achievement."

"Certainly better than the honorable mention I got," Carolyn added. "However, I'll take that, and if we come back next year, I'll do better." She frowned. "Oh, wait. With Mr. Boudreau in jail, will the cook-off even continue?"

"I guess we'll have to wait and see," Phyllis said. She looked over at Eve, who was sitting with them in lawn chairs in front of the War Wagon as darkness settled down. "Are you all right?"

"Why would you ask?" Eve said. "Because Hiram turned out to be a cold-blooded murderer? Dear, I was just flirting with the man. There was nothing serious about it. I'm well past the point of ever getting serious again."

Phyllis wasn't sure she believed that, but Eve did seem to be taking what had happened in stride. She had known Boudreau only a few days, hadn't done anything more than dance and flirt with him, and besides . . . as it turned out, he wasn't an oil millionaire after all.

With a rumble of gravel under its wheels, Chuck's Jeep came along the aisle between rows of parked travel trailers and motor homes. The young constable brought the vehicle to a halt in front of the War Wagon. He climbed out, moving a little stiffly from the bandages wrapped around his torso.

He nodded to Phyllis and the others and said, "I wanted to make sure you folks were doing all right after all the excitement this morning."

"You're the one who was injured, Chuck," Phyllis said. "The rest of us are fine."

"Well, I'm glad to hear it."

Sam said, "You're lucky that girl McKayla had a crush on you and was followin' you around, Constable. If she hadn't seen Boudreau about to go after you again with that knife, things might've been a lot worse."

"Yes, that . . . certainly came in handy,

didn't it?" Chuck looked like this part of the conversation made him uncomfortable, and well it should, Phyllis thought. He had promised to keep his distance from Mc-Kayla, even it meant resigning his constable's position, moving to the county seat, and trying to get a job with the sheriff's department. Phyllis thought Sergeant Culbertson might put in a good word for him.

Chuck went on, "I guess you'll be heading home in the morning?"

"That's right," Phyllis said.

"If you need anything between now and then, let me know, okay?" Chuck smiled, climbed back into the Jeep, and drove off, waving farewell as he went.

"Nice young fella," Sam commented. "Hope he gets all his problems worked out."

"He just needs to be patient," Phyllis said. Sam looked at her and nodded in understanding. McKayla would be of age in a few years. If she still felt the same way then, she and Chuck might turn out to have something real.

"Uh-oh," Sam said then as he glanced past Phyllis. "Look who's comin'."

Texas Ranger Sergeant Martin Culbertson walked along the row of travel trailers and motor homes, and as always, his stride was purposeful. He was headed right toward them, too, Phyllis noted.

"Evening, ladies," Culbertson greeted them. He took his hat off this time. "Mr. Fletcher."

"We don't have an extra chair," Sam said, "or I'd tell you to pull up a seat, Sergeant. Be glad to get you a beer . . . or a bowl of chili."

Culbertson smiled and shook his head. "No, thanks. I just thought I'd stop by and let you know that we've gotten a full statement from Hiram Boudreau admitting that he sabotaged the propane tank on Hammersmith's motor home. He confessed to killing Harlan Anders, too, but he's insisting that Anders' children were in on it with him. He even said it was their idea, but I'm not sure if I believe that." The Ranger's broad shoulders rose and fell in a shrug. "But it'll be up to the courts to hash all that out. The important thing as far as I'm concerned is that the Hammersmith case is cleared." He cocked his head at Phyllis. "You can chalk up another one."

"I'm not keeping score," she said.

"But if she was, she'd be undefeated," Carolyn added.

Phyllis said, "I suppose Boudreau confessed because Nick shot that footage of him trying to kill Constable Snyder. With evidence like that, and with everything he'd already said, he must have thought there was no point in denying the rest of it."

"We'll build a good case against him, don't worry about that," Culbertson said. "And that TV lady will get some good ratings out of the whole deal."

"And that's what's most important . . . to her."

Sam said, "The most important thing to me is that I'm not gonna be hauled off to jail, so I get to keep on spendin' my time with my friends and family." He looked at Phyllis, Carolyn, and Eve. "With this bunch, it's pretty much one and the same."

Culbertson turned his hat over in his hands and said, "I'd wish you luck, Mr. Fletcher . . . but from what I can see, you've already got plenty of it."

He smiled at Phyllis, and she felt her face warming in a way that had nothing to do with the heat of the day still lingering in the air. She was glad when there was a boom nearby that made everyone look around.

It was no explosion this time, but rather a rocket that rose gracefully into the air and then burst in a brilliant panoply of light. More fireworks arched into the heavens above Cactus Bluff and lit them up, and Phyllis sat and watched them with a smile on her face.

"It's gonna be mighty good to see Buck again," Sam said as he steered the pickup along the tree-lined street in Weatherford. It was late the next day, and another long, wearying drive was behind them. But all four of them were looking forward to being home.

Sam hadn't wanted to board his beloved Dalmatian, so one of the neighbors had agreed to come in and feed Buck every day. He had a good doghouse on the back porch, plenty of shade in the back yard, and a multitude of squirrels to chase for exercise and excitement. The neighbor's son was happy to come over every day and throw a ball for Buck to chase, too. Still, this was the first time he and Sam had been apart, so Sam had worried about him.

Now the house was in sight, nestled among the tall old trees, and Phyllis felt a surge of warmth go through her. There was nothing quite like coming home again.

Sam pulled into the driveway and hit the remote to raise the garage door. It rumbled up as he stopped the pickup and the four travelers climbed out.

"My own bed is going to feel wonderful tonight!" Carolyn said.

Phyllis went through the garage to the door that opened into the kitchen. She stuck her key in the lock and turned it, then stiffened as she realized something.

"Sam," she called quietly as she turned to him, "this door was unlocked."

Sam frowned. "Maybe Mrs. Duncan left it that way when she came over to feed Buck."

"She wouldn't have had any reason to come out here. Anyway, she's very reliable and responsible. That just doesn't seem like something she'd do."

Sam reached for the knob. "Best let me go in first."

"I can call Mike —"

"No need for that," Sam said. "You don't want to worry the boy for no reason." He turned the knob, eased the door open, and stepped quietly into the kitchen.

If there was a problem inside, Phyllis wasn't going to let him face it alone. She was close behind him as he started through the kitchen. Carolyn and Eve trailed her, a little farther back where they could still reach the door in a hurry.

Then, completely unexpectedly, a female voice called from the living room, "Hey, we're in here! I saw the pickup pull in."

Sam's back straightened. He turned his

279

head and glanced at Phyllis, and she could tell that he was utterly surprised. But he hesitated only a second before he strode on into the living room and then stopped with Phyllis at his heels. She looked past him and saw a young woman with bright blue hair sitting on the sofa with Buck, who barked happily and rushed to his master as soon as he saw Sam. He jumped up to rest his paws on Sam's chest, and seemingly without thinking, Sam rubbed and scratched the dog's ears as Buck squirmed joyously.

The blue-haired girl stood up, grinned, and said to Sam, "What's the matter, Gramps? Aren't you glad to see your favorite granddaughter?"

RECIPES

SAM'S SMOKIN' RED

Ingredients

3 lbs. cubed trimmed tri-tip roast, 1/4 inch cubes

2 tablespoons of beef fat

1 cup chopped white onion

4–6 cloves garlic, minced

1 cup Bare Bones Classic Beef Bone broth

1 cup Bare Bones Classic Chicken Bone broth

1 16-ounce Can-Muir Glen organic tomato sauce

1st Spices

1 teaspoon Mexican oregano

1 tablespoon American paprika

1 1/2 teaspoons onion powder

1 teaspoon garlic powder

2 teaspoon beef granules

1 teaspoon chicken granules

1/2 teaspoon seasoned salt

1 tablespoon New Mexico chili powder

2nd Spices

3 teaspoons ground cumin
1/2 teaspoon garlic powder
1/2 teaspoon seasoned salt
1 1/2 tablespoon Gebhardt chili powder
1 1/2 tablespoons Texas style chili powder
1/2 tablespoons New Mexico hot ground chili pepper
1/2 tablespoon New Mexico light chili powder

3rd Spices

2 teaspoons Texas style chili powder
1 teaspoon ground cumin
1/4 teaspoon garlic powder

Tabasco sauce (as needed for heat)

Directions

Brown meat in 2 tablespoons of beef fat. Place meat in colander and drain off oil. Rinse meat with water and return meat to pot.

Add broths, tomato sauce, and 1st spices. Cook approximately 2 hours, add water if necessary, stirring occasionally. Chili has a tendency to burn on the bottom if not stirred enough. It depends on the thickness of your pot how often you will need to stir, a thicker pot can sit a little longer between stirs. (I stir mine every 10-15 minutes.) Cook longer if meat is not tender.

30 minutes before finished, add 2nd spices.

15 minutes before finished, add 3rd spices.

Add seasoned salt for taste. For heat, add Tabasco to taste.

Cooking Time – 3 Hours

GLUTEN FREE OAT MUFFINS

Ingredients
1 1/2 cups old-fashioned oats
1 teaspoon baking powder
1/4 teaspoon baking soda
1 cup mashed ripe bananas (about 2)
2 eggs
2 tablespoons room-temp natural almond butter (no salt or sugar added)
2 tablespoons honey
1/4 cup milk
1/4 cup grated carrot
1/4 cup peeled and grated apple, thoroughly blotted dry

Directions:
Preheat oven to 350 degrees. Spray a 12-cup muffin pan with nonstick spray.

Place oats in a small blender or food processor, and pulse until reduced to the consistency of a coarse flour.

In a large bowl, combine ground oats, baking powder, and baking soda.

In a medium-large bowl, combine all remaining ingredients except apple and carrot. Stir until uniform.

Add contents of the medium-large bowl to the large bowl, and mix until well blended.

Fold in apple and carrot. Evenly fill muffin pan with batter.

Bake until a toothpick inserted into the center of a muffin comes out clean, 20-22 minutes.

Makes 12 muffins

PHYLLIS'S GINGER CITRUS TEA

Ingredients

1 quart water
1/2–1 cup granulated sugar
1 tablespoon of grated ginger
4 tea bags or 1 family size tea bag (4 tablespoons loose leaf)
juice of 1 lime
juice of 1 lemon

Directions

In a medium sauce pan, add the water, sugar, grated ginger. Bring to a boil on medium heat. Stir occasionally.

Once boiling, add the tea bag(s) and remove from heat. Allow tea to steep for 5 minutes. Strain tea to remove tea leaves/bag(s) and ginger pieces.

While the tea is brewing, juice the lime and lemon.

In a pitcher, combine the tea, lemon juice, and lime juice. Stir.

Served chilled or over ice.

Serves 4

Note: Ginger has a lot of health benefits, but it can be difficult to grate with a box grater. It's best to use a microplane grater that is designed to be used with ginger. Freezing ginger makes it more solid and easier to grate.

SPICY CORN WAFFLES

Ingredients
1 1/4 cups yellow cornmeal
1 3/4 cups all-purpose flour
1 teaspoon Gebhardt chili powder
1 tablespoon baking powder
1 teaspoon sugar
1 teaspoon salt
2 cups milk
3 tablespoons vegetable oil
2 large eggs
1/2 cup chopped jalapeño peppers
Sam's Smokin' Red Chili
shredded cheddar, for garnish
sour cream, for garnish
chopped green onions, for garnish

Directions
Preheat waffle iron according to manufacturer's instructions.

In a large bowl, combine cornmeal, flour,

chili powder, baking powder, sugar, and salt. Add milk, oil, eggs, and jalapeño peppers, stirring until smooth. Pour batter onto hot waffle iron and bake in batches. Set aside and keep warm.

Serve with Sam's Smokin' Red Chili. Garnish with shredded cheddar, sour cream and chopped fresh green onions. Note: To keep the waffles from soaking up too much of the chili, put grated cheese on the waffle, and then add chili.

10 to 12 servings.

CHILI GLUTEN FREE LASAGNA

Ingredients
12 no-boil gluten free lasagna noodles
2 cups left over chili
1 egg
1 3/4 cups ricotta cheese
4 cups cheddar cheese, grated
3 cups chunky salsa
1 tablespoon green onions, chopped, optional
sour cream, optional
1 bunch fresh cilantro, for garnish

Directions
Preheat oven to 350° F and lightly grease a 9×13 baking dish.

In a medium bowl, mix egg with ricotta cheese until well combined. Set aside.

Place 4 lasagna noodles in bottom of baking dish. Spread 1/3 of ricotta over noodles, then evenly spoon 1/3 of chili over ricotta. Evenly spread 1/3 of salsa over chili, then layer 1/3 of cheddar cheese over salsa. Repeat steps, finishing with cheddar cheese.

Cover with foil and bake for 30-40 minutes, or until lasagna is heated through. Take off foil and bake for 10 more minutes.

Let cool 5-10 minutes, top with sour cream and fresh cilantro, (optional), serve and enjoy!

Serves 6-8

CHEESY CHILI
SHEPHERD'S PIE

Ingredients

6 large potatoes, peeled and quartered
1 package (8 ounces) cream cheese, softened
1 cup (4 ounces) shredded cheddar cheese
1/2 cup sour cream
1/3 cup chopped onion
1 large egg
2 teaspoons salt
1/2 teaspoon pepper
3 cups of chili
1 can pinto beans drained and rinsed
additional shredded cheddar cheese, optional

Directions

Place potatoes in a large saucepan; cover with water, add lid and bring to a boil. Cook for 20-25 minutes or until tender. Drain.

In a bowl, mash potatoes. Add cream

cheese, cheddar cheese, sour cream, onion, egg, salt and pepper; beat until fluffy.

Mix chili and beans and put in the bottom of a greased 2-qt. baking dish. Cover with the cheesy mashed potatoes. Cover casserole and bake at 350° for 40-45 minutes or until heated through. Sprinkle with additional cheese if desired.

Serves 6

CHILI POTATO CAKES

Ingredients

4 potatoes par-boiled (barely soft) diced in small cubes
1 teaspoon salt
1 teaspoon sugar
1/2 teaspoon chili powder
1/8 teaspoon black pepper
1/3 cup flour
2 tablespoons skim milk powder
1 teaspoon butter softened
1 beaten egg
1 cup chili
1 cup grated cheddar cheese

Directions

Combine all ingredients except chili and cheese in a bowl until mixed.

Freeze mixture for half hour to firm it.

Place potato mixture between two pieces of

wax or parchment paper and roll out to 1/4 inch.

Freeze until solid.

Cut into squares or other shapes, and fry in hot oil.

Add chili on top of hash brown and garnish with cheese.

Serves 4-6

ABOUT THE AUTHOR

Livia J. Washburn has been a professional writer for more than thirty years. She received the Private Eye Writers of America Award and the American Mystery Award for her first mystery, *Wild Night,* written under the name L. J. Washburn, and she was nominated for a Spur Award by the Western Writers of America for a novel written with her husband, James Reasoner. Her short story "Panhandle Freight" was nominated for a Peacemaker Award by the Western Fictioneers, and her story *Charlie's Pie* won. She lives with her husband in a small Texas town, where she is constantly experimenting with new recipes. Her two grown daughters are both teachers in her hometown, and she is very proud of them.